1

PROLOGUE – CARTER

ADDISON MAKES ME FEEL LIKE A BLUSHING TEENAGER with his first crush. The innocent Catholic girl is oblivious to the thoughts running through my head as she sits beside me in the Uber. She's aware I like her. She'd have to be stupid to not notice that, and she's anything but. If she were any other girl, she'd have visited my bed by now. But Addison is different, and I knew that from the first time I noticed her across the bar at Duke's.

She'd been with Bennett's wife, Scarlett, and I'd wondered if she was putting on the shyness. Sutton the asshole had decided to keep her company that night. I should have ignored them, but I hadn't been able to. There was something about Addison that had me searching her out.

I'm being pathetic.

My eyes drop to her lap, where her nervousness is evident in the tightening of her fingers.

With a small smile on my lips, I reach forward and pry her fingers apart. I place her palm on top of mine and show her how to intertwine our fingers. Addison releases a short breath and quickly meets my gaze. I squeeze our hands. "Don't worry," I say, and dipping closer to her ear add, "Enjoy." A shudder runs through her, and I pause when I see goose bumps coating her skin.

Needing a taste to take home with me, I press an open-mouthed kiss to her neck.

"Oh," slips free of her mouth like a sigh.

We're a few minutes from her address, and wanting to end our evening on a note of wickedness, I nibble on her delicate earlobe. "If one kiss makes you tremble"—I brush my lips down her neck and back up—"imagine what it would feel like to have me kiss you all over."

Her breathing is rapid when the driver pulls up outside her apartment building. Addison doesn't notice where we are or that we've even stopped as she holds my gaze.

"You are a dangerous man, Carter," she whispers, her voice full of seriousness. "I want to do things with you that I shouldn't even think about."

Stunned, I blink a few times and find her already on the sidewalk before I realize it. I stumble out after her, leaving the door open so the driver doesn't leave without me.

I reach for her, but she steps back and looks around. "I can't. Not here," she hisses. "There are eyes everywhere."

"When?" I beg and don't give a shit. I want to see this girl again and again and again.

"I can't think," she mutters, taking a step toward me.

"Addison," a sharp voice snaps.

Addison jumps and runs toward the voice.

Maureen!

Disappearing inside the apartment building, Addison gives me a glance of longing over her shoulder before the other girl ushers her into the elevator.

Not sure how long I stare after her, the driver

eventually clears his throat loud enough for me to hear him.

On the way back to my place, my head is full of the girl. Of the way she trembled when I touched her with my lips. Of the way she tasted in the too brief kiss on her neck. Of the way she will taste when we're alone in the dark.

Swallowing hard, I rein in my thoughts before I embarrass myself in the Uber. It's so not the place to get a hard-on.

Go slow, Carter.

2

CARTER

Blood pumps though my veins as I work up a sweat lifting weights. I'm a lazy ass really and hate spending time in the gym. Boring is how I think of it.

Across the way Ivan relishes the strain and the repetition of training. The large Russian defender likes order. I wish I did, maybe then I wouldn't be confused about moving forward with Addison.

Me and my big mouth asked her to move in with me. I offered her the guest room with its own private bathroom. I thought saving her from having to move in with Maureen would be better.

Maureen has been a bitch to Addison. It was Maureen's own fault she got in an accident. The girl should have been watching what she was doing instead of spying on Addison and me.

But for whatever reason, Addison refused my offer and decided to move into the apartment with Maureen that their parents had rented.

I know my girl is unhappy, and maybe she said yes to her parents and no to me because of her faith. Either way it hurt and left me disgruntled. I'm not sure what to make of it.

Whatever it was, I plan on being there for her, if she'll let me. I want to show her I won't bail regardless of the obstacles put in front of us.

My own fear is that she might one day listen to her parents and friend. They don't like me because I'm not a nice Catholic boy. They probably mean virgin.

Bryson sits on the bench opposite me, no doubt waiting for me to finish to bend my ear about something. For a carefree guy, he has looked troubled a time or two.

Using him as an excuse to finish my workout, I drop the weight home and raise a brow. "Why are you here so early?"

"Nice to see you too." He lies back along the workout bench with a heavy sigh.

"I'm bored," he comments. "I've never been bored before, and I find it frustrating."

Bryson bored, that does surprise me. "How are you bored? The girls are always after you."

"I don't know what I want. I was perfectly fine and now everything is upside down. I'm unsettled and don't know why or what to do about it."

"Until you know why, I don't think you can do anything."

I wipe the sweat off my face with a towel and eye Ivan training. "He's dedicated."

"Has nothing else to do." Bry shrugs.

"You need to hang out with Ivan." I Smirk. "You said it yourself, he has nothing else to do and you're bored. Together I'm sure you two will think of something."

Bryson eyes me warily. "He'll think I'm hitting on him."

I snort in amusement. "I'm sure he's aware of how much you like tits and pussy by now."

He throws me a disgusted look. "Talking about tits and pussy, I haven't seen Addison around in a while."

I shoot him a glare. "Don't talk about her like that." I pause. "She's been busy moving in with that girl." I can't bring myself to use her name because

I'm so annoyed at the way Addison was manipulated.

"You need to marry the girl and move her in with you. Her parents can't say anything then because I'm guessing they are all no sex before marriage shit."

"It's not only her parents." I shake off the negative thoughts. "Let's talk about something else. I need fuel. Burger and fries sound really good."

Ivan curses beside me. "You need something healthy. Organic."

Bry winces behind Ivan's back.

"I've got a better idea. Why don't Bry and I show you the best place to eat? You'll forget all about that healthy crap. I promise."

"Nyet." Ivan shakes his head. "I have been to that place before."

Bryson snickers. "I have it on good authority that they have a new waitress by the name of Payton Collins." He crosses his arms.

The big defenseman turns to stone.

"Who is Payton Collins?" I ask, curious.

"A beautiful girl," Ivan states. "We go and eat." He's off with Bryson following behind him with a huge grin on his face.

My stomach growls. "Hold up." I run after them.

After all, it was my idea to begin with. "I'll meet you there."

My head goes straight to wanting Addison to join us. I chew on the decision until I'm at my truck. I have nothing to lose, so I shoot off a text to my girl. It's read instantly and then I see the dots indicating she's replying, but nothing comes through. I debate calling but refrain. She doesn't like me calling because it's awkward for her, which I find irritating.

Once or twice after we first met, I wondered about the attraction I felt toward her. And if it would be worth pursuing. I decided it was. Recently, I've wondered again what the hell I'm doing. We hardly see each other and when we do, she is in a rush to get home.

Bryson isn't the only one out of sorts.

When I arrive at the mom-and-pop diner, Ivan and Bry already have a table.

Once I'm seated, I recognize the shy girl serving us. She's been in the executive box during games. I smile. "Hi, Payton. How are you today?"

"I'm fine, thanks, Carter. Hi, Bryson, Ivan." Her blush deepens as she looks at the Russian, no doubt his stare is embarrassing her.

I cough, and when that doesn't work, I kick Ivan under the table.

"He doesn't speak English." I grin and get a very dark glare.

"Glupaya yeblya!" Ivan curses under his breath. "How long have you worked here?" he blurts.

Bryson snickers.

I grab a menu from the table and hide my amusement behind it.

"Not long," Payton says. "What can I get you today?"

We give Payton our orders, and I turn my full attention to Ivan when she walks away. He doesn't look so happy about it. "So, how did you meet the lovely Payton?"

Ivan glares and sags before us. "She came to the family day. With her boyfriend." He scowls. "I do not like him."

"Hmm. You don't like him because he has Payton or is it something more?"

"He is not nice man."

"Why don't you invite her to have coffee with you?" Bryson suggests.

"My visa runs out soon. Wyatt. He tries to get it

extended, but Russia does not listen. I do not want to be her friend then leave."

Our food arrives.

Munching on my burger, it feels like cardboard going down. I had no idea my teammate was having problems staying in the country. What to do about it though?

Halfway through eating my mouth drops open in surprise as Addison walks through the door. The smile she throws my way lifts my mood and I grin like a fool.

Ivan clears his throat, then a smirk forms on his face, and Bryson looks more amused than I've seen him before.

"Fuck you both," I hiss under my breath.

Ivan snorts, and I kick him under the table. I want to smack the smirk from Bryson's face.

"She's mine," I growl.

Bryson chuckles. "I'm aware."

"Thanks for the invite," she says.

Ivan shoves over and she drops down beside him. Payton suddenly appears, which causes Ivan the big lug to stare as though he hasn't seen her before. His girl blushes a lovely shade of red as she glances between Addison and Ivan.

The bulb goes off.

"Payton." I draw her gaze. "I'd like you to meet my girlfriend, Addison."

"Oh," she whispers. "I'll grab some coffee."

Addison frowns. "What was that about?"

Bryson and I point at Ivan, who blushes.

"You like her?" She smiles softly at Ivan. "Why don't you ask her out?"

"Nyet." He shoves his plate away and puts his head down. Moments later he ushers Addison up. "Bry, we leave."

Byson throws a dark glare after Ivan. "What bug crawled up his ass?" He shoves out of the booth, and I move and sit with Addison.

"Are you hungry?"

Coffee is placed in front of her.

"No. Coffee is fine. I start work soon."

"Drink up and I'll walk you." I lean in and kiss her cheek. "You smell good." I hover at her neck and smile as blush crawls up her skin. "Am I making you hot?" I move closer until our sides are touching, my hand on her thigh.

She murmurs a soft moan, which goes straight to my dick. I push my luck slightly and slide my hand beneath her dress. Smooth naked skin is under my fingertips. I stroke further and although it's subtle, I notice the shift in her as her legs fall open. A weird noise leaves her lips.

I quickly pull my hand away and meet her glazed eyes. Extremely frustrated, my dick throbs in my sweats. I'm not going to be moving anytime soon.

"You like me touching you." I sit back and finish my coffee before I grab her up and make use of the restroom to finish myself off.

"Yes," she says softly. "I like it more than I've been taught."

Nodding, I hide my thoughts on her upbringing and urge her to finish her drink.

3

ADDISON

I love how Carter makes me feel from just his touch. I do want more but don't know how to ask. I'm not one for blurting out things of intimacy, so I'm feeling a bit lost.

My friends tell me to go for it, but I don't think they realize I'm clueless. I mean, I know what goes where, but it's everything else I'm a bit lost with. Like how do we get to that part?

Molly had mentioned how much she loves Camden's mouth between her legs. Is that normal? I should have asked her. If I weren't too shy, I would have.

"You're a lovely shade of red," Carter comments. "Feel like sharing?"

We're walking toward the library, well, more like strolling. My hand is engulfed in his while he eyes me. A smirk graces his handsome face.

"Should I guess what you're thinking about, then?"

"It might be best not to," I admit and chuckle.

Clearing his throat, he says, "Molly has tickets for tonight's game." He gives me a hopeful look, and the last thing I want to do is say no.

"I want to be there," I say, and his face falls, which he quickly hides. Coming to a stop, I take both his hands into mine. "I really do want to be there, Carter. I have a dinner thing with my parents at the church. I'd much rather watch you." I kiss his hands and hold them against my mouth. "You're rather nice to watch."

He smiles.

"I spend a lot of time with my eyes on your legs and butt."

He bursts out laughing and this time he really is amused. "What about this face?"

"Oh, I look at that all the time. I love the sweaty look. Fuels my imagination."

He opens and closes his mouth, and I start walking again.

"I thought you should know."

"Hmm." He drapes an arm around my waist.

"Don't tell me all your guilty pleasures right now, otherwise I'll be an embarrassment."

It takes me a moment to get what he means, and when I do, my eyes drop straight to his groin. "Oh!"

He groans. "Tell me about this dinner."

"I'd rather not. I'm so not looking forward to it."

"Then why go?"

"Because I said I would." I shrug. "My parents accepted on my behalf. It's one dinner. I'll go, plaster a smile on my face, eat and then leave. I told them it's the last time, and if they accept an invitation for me again, then they can explain my absence."

I can tell by the tightness of his face that he's unhappy with how I'm treated. It's nothing new and a bit of a bone of contention between us.

"What about the game tonight? Shouldn't you be training or something?" I change the topic, and he glances my way, letting me know he's aware of what I'm doing.

He lets me. "I'll have a light skate when I get back and then Coach will be giving us a talking to." He grins. "I know we take the fun out of him, but he's a really good coach."

"I've heard him shouting in Russian; he's very animated." I sigh. "I'll message Molly and tell her I'll try and sneak away and come to the game. I want to be there for you, Carter. Wearing your shirt and screaming your name."

His eyes go hooded. "I can think of more pleasurable ways to have you screaming my name." His brows wiggling make me laugh, and I become utterly spontaneous and throw my arms around his neck and hold on tight.

Carter's big, strong arms come around me and hold me close. He nuzzles into the curve of my neck, moaning into my ear. "You feel amazing in my arms."

"I feel safe in yours. Safe and comfortable," I admit. Being more daring, I rub against his arousal digging into me. "And hot and bothered too."

He swallows hard and slowly releases me, his forehead resting against mine. "If you can't get away, will you come to my place afterward?"

"Yes."

My face is suddenly cupped in his large hands as he brings his mouth to mine for a much too brief kiss. "You taste delicious."

I lick my lips and enjoy the look in his gaze as he watches. My lips twitch up into a smile. "It may get late, but I'll be there."

"Good." He coughs and takes my hand. "Let's get you to work before you're late."

The library is across the street. "I love this place. Being surrounded by books. Millions and billions of pages with written words." I smile as we move closer. "Imagine the people who first came here back in the 1800s. I often wonder about what their occupations would have been. It intrigues me."

"You light up when you talk about the library. It's lovely to see." Carter presses another quick kiss to my lips. "I hate to rush you, but I need to get to the arena."

"It's okay. I'm glad we got to spend a bit of time together." I give him a brief hug, and rush toward the entrance, waving over my shoulder.

He blows me a kiss and disappears.

I'm still smiling as I walk into the building, shooting smiles to people I know as I breeze past.

A harried looking Yvette rushes over the second she spots me. "Claire and Diane are out sick," she says. "I would have called you in, but I knew you'd be in soon." She shrugs, looking apologetic.

"Give me a few minutes to lock my purse away and then I'm all yours."

"Thank you." She leans closer. "Those girls have

no idea that I'm aware they went out drinking *very* late last night. Tsk. I may be old, but I wasn't born yesterday."

"Don't worry. I'll be quick." Before she can say any more, I stride through the library to the secure room where the staff lockers are kept.

I toss everything inside mine, lock it up, and head out on to the floor.

I love my job.

4

CARTER

BRINGING TO THE ICE GOOD SPIRITS AFTER SEEING Addison and her promise to meet me later tonight, I feel like I'm sailing across the ice.

My friends give me knowing smirks but who cares. I'm happy after having doubts and feel ready to take on the world.

Her touch, her smile, the way she gives me her undivided attention, there isn't anything I don't like. Well, maybe her parents. Control freaks is what they are, and it bothers me a lot more than I let on to Addison. They dislike me, which doesn't help Addison being with me.

Thud!

Flat on my back, I blink and focus on the ceiling above me.

What the fuck happened?

"You okay?" Bennett offers me a hand and hauls my ass from the ice. "Concentrate on practice, yeah?" He grins. "There would have been a lot of pain if Ivan hadn't shoved you out of the way."

"Shit!" I shake my head and release a long breath.

Coach gives me a dark glare, causing me to wince. I'm not going to get away unscathed after all.

Bryson skates over. "I take it lunch went well." The asshole smirks.

I grin. "Very well." My eyes drift toward Ivan, who gives me a rude gesture.

"How real is that shit with Ivan?" I ask Bry.

"Very real. Wyatt is trying to sort it out. The main issue though is the Russians want Ivan for themselves. So it isn't looking good."

A string of Russian, no doubt curse words, comes out of Coach Van's mouth as he approaches me and Bry.

Deflecting his thoughts, I tell Van, "We were talking about what's going on with Ivan."

"That is not good. He is a good man and wants to stay here. This team is family. But Ivan, he will go because he is Russian, and his mother and sister are there.

"Things could turn bad for them if he refuses. Wyatt tries to pull strings to bring them here. It is not working."

"Is there anything we can do?" Bryson asks.

Camden, Bennett, Theo, and Sutton join us.

Coach snaps his fingers. "They need to marry an American! Ivan can marry that girl. Anya can marry Bryson."

Bry narrows his eyes. "And you, Coach, can marry the mother, *da?*"

Snickers erupt, annoying Van. It doesn't shut us up though. I think I'm more amused at the thought of Bryson being the groom in an arranged marriage than Coach.

As we trudge from the ice, Wyatt appears. "I see you are having fun at Van's expense again."

Ethan joins us, having heard the tail end of our conversation with Van. "It was suggested Van marries Ivan's mother."

Wyatt gives us a look and says, "Oh my God! I never thought of that." He does an about-face and rushes off.

We greet Ethan, who is still out because of his broken ankle. If it weren't for Riley, he'd be a bear.

"I missed who got volunteered to marry the sister." Ethan glances at us unwed guys.

Theo laughs. "That would be Bryson." He delights in the announcement, thumping Bry on the back.

Bryson shudders. "Fuck you! I'm not marring a female Ivan."

Ethan laughs. "She's no Ivan. Think... Hmm, I'm not sure. She's nothing like Ivan anyway."

I don't miss the interest Theo quickly hides. I glance at Ethan. "She hot?"

"She's tiny compared to her brother. Looks sweet and yes, she is hot, not that I will ever admit that in front of my wife."

"Joking aside," I say, "is there really nothing we can do to help him stay?"

"Wyatt doesn't tell me much because he knows I'm friends with you guys."

"Just because you're an old married man doesn't mean you have to be jealous of us single guys," says Theo.

Ethan rolls his eyes and falls in beside me. "Riley tells me Addison ended up moving in with that girl."

"Yeah. I offered her a place to stay. Own room and

everything. She thought it best to stay with Maureen."
I shrug even though it pisses me off. "I think she feels
guilty for what happened to Maureen. She tells me
she doesn't."

"Then if Addison means something to you, I guess
you support her until she's ready to move on with
you."

"And what if she doesn't move on?"

Ethan smirks. "She will. I'm an expert on these
things now."

Sutton snorts. "Like hell you are."

"I told Riley you'd end up with Hailee." Ethan
grins. "I was right too. I didn't see Noah with your
sister though."

Scowling, Sutton says, "He is not with my sister.
They're friends."

I grin. "Just like I'm friends with Addison, huh?"

I get the finger.

"I'll catch you after the game." Ethan hobbles off.

I watch him go and realize he's happy. Being
married has changed him, and I'm happy for him.

"Carter," is screeched loudly that my eardrums
grumble seconds before a woman with an overpow-
ering scent jumps me. "I've missed you."

I have no clue who this clinging woman is. Taking

hold of her wrists, I untangle myself. I recognize her and my heart sinks. She's a puck bunny who I happen to have an intimate knowledge of.

"Um." I hesitate.

"Lucy," she supplies. "I haven't seen you in Duke's for a while."

"How did you get in here?" I glance around, but no help is coming.

"Don't be silly. I know everyone." Her hands press on my chest and slowly creep upward.

I tell myself not to look down at her amazing tits. I do remember those, so does my dick.

What the fuck am I doing sporting wood with this woman's tits jiggling in my face?

Shaking my head, I step back. "You need to leave," I demand.

"Come to Duke's after the game. I'll help you celebrate." She wiggles her tits.

Swallowing hard, I move quickly away. "I'll see you around," I shout over my shoulder.

I escape into the locker room, where the mood is solemn before the game. It always is until Coach gives us all his wisdom. Most game days it works, and we come out victorious.

I drop into the seat at my cubby and once again

find myself wondering which direction I want my life to go in.

Addison is always the last person I think about before sleep claims me and the first person I think of when I wake.

I'm frustrated. That's what is going on with me. That's why I noticed Lucy's tits. I mean, she had them hanging out. I'm a guy. We look.

Fuck!

Perhaps I'm the one who needs to spend time in a confessional, or maybe I need a shit ton of holy water to wash my eyes out.

I love Addison.

5

ADDISON

"Addison, how lovely to see you here this evening."

I hide my misery behind a smile. "Thank you, Mrs. Long."

My mother's mouth tightens at my lack of greeting. Mrs. Long doesn't seem bothered, only my parents.

It's going to be a long evening with them hovering at my elbow. I feel as though I'm being tag teamed by them. Makes me wonder whether Maureen caught me shoving a dress into my purse this evening. She'd have no trouble informing my mother.

I'm not surprised Carter gets annoyed with how difficult it is to spend any time together. I hate it too.

I've tried to make light of it recently so he doesn't get exasperated to the point that he says no more and he's done with me.

A sharp elbow in my side pushes me forward and into the man my parents want me to marry. Jeremy Tyson.

His face lights up and he coughs to clear his throat while a flush appears on his cheeks. It isn't his fault our parents have encouraged our friendship. I feel sorry for him, and myself.

I return his smile. "Jeremy, how are you?"

"Well." He shuffles his feet. "You?"

"Good."

My father mutters something I don't catch under his breath.

"Would you like to join me?" Jeremy asks.

"Yes," I say with relief, ignoring the painful pinch my mother gives me in warning to watch my tongue.

Jeremy leads me through the church hall toward the end of one of the tables. A lot of people are expected tonight, so the room has been turned into a dining hall.

"I'm glad you're here. It will make tonight more bearable." Jeremy leans closer. "Is Maureen not coming?" he whispers.

"No." I frown. "I never even asked if her parents were bringing her."

Chuckling, Jeremy says, "I don't blame you for not bothering. That girl is bad."

Even though I have no interest in marrying Jeremy, I do like him as a friend. Probably because I'm aware of his feelings for someone else. We both have secrets.

"I don't suppose you'd cover for me after the meal?"

He grins. "We will cover for each other. Say we're going for a walk."

I'm not sure either of our parents will fall for that, but it's worth a try.

"How come you always get dragged into these things? Your parents are more lenient with you."

"The food." He grins. "It's easier just going along. I'm the perfect son." He winces. "If only they knew."

Feeling sad for him and myself, I take his hand. "We need to find strength to break away from our families' expectations. Why shouldn't we be happy, Jeremy? Maureen wasn't happy, and because of me, she is now in a wheelchair."

"No." He strengthens his hold. "Maureen is responsible for what happened. You had no idea she was following you until the accident happened. She is to blame. She stepped in front of the car. Do not blame yourself."

He pauses and then continues, "Is that why you are now living with the dreadful girl? Because you feel guilty?"

I slowly nod, and admit, "Carter wanted me to move in with him. He offered me his guest room. I should have gotten some backbone and agreed. I don't think he's happy that I didn't."

Jeremy sighs. "Chris wants me to move in too. It's difficult, isn't it? Our hearts want one thing, but our family loyalty makes us do something else." He covers our hands with his free one.

"I'm so glad our parents put us together. It's good having you to talk to."

"Yes." He quickly glances around, his eyes full of mirth when he meets mine. "Our mothers have stupid grins on their faces. I think we should start using each other as excuses more. What do you say?"

Relieved that this could sort things out with Carter, I grin. "I'm totally in favor of this plan of yours."

"Oh good!" His smile stretches from ear to ear. "This is going to be fun. Chris will be delighted."

"Carter will be too."

Maureen will be a problem.

"I know what you are thinking. That girl can no longer move as fast." He cringes. "I'm not a horrid person, at least I don't think I am."

"You're not. We're both trapped and need to protect ourselves and what we want from now on." I realize we're still holding hands. "Kiss my hand," I whisper. "Make it look like you're enamored with me."

Smiling with amusement twinkling in his eyes, Jeremy puts on a wonderful show.

Just in time too as my mother appears.

"Let's sit together." She smiles.

"We'd like that, wouldn't we, Addison?" Jeremy squeezes my fingers before letting go. "If you'll excuse me for one moment, please."

My mother sits beside me. "I am happy you are getting along with Jeremy. He is a nice boy."

"I agree."

My mother is delighted by my response. "Has he asked you on a date?"

"We were just discussing that when you interrupted. Maybe we will take a walk after dinner."

My mother frowns.

I distract her. "Where has Father gone?"

"To discuss business with John. He's no doubt sneaking a shot of whiskey behind my back."

My father likes his drink. Unfortunately, it doesn't like him. So my mother telling me what he is doing is a warning to avoid any confrontation.

It's difficult to decide whether it's more of an excuse these days to keep me in line.

Nevertheless, I have no intention of them finding out about my planned evening.

All through the meal I keep up a polite and steady conversation with Jeremy, us both trying to avoid clock-watching.

It's a relief when we remove our own plates and utensils. We each in turn rinse the plates used and then put them into one of the two dishwashers available.

Jeremy appears at my elbow. "Ready?"

I nod and turn to find my father standing over me. "We're going for a walk," I say, hoping my voice sounds better than a small quiver.

"Don't worry, Mr. James, I will walk Addison home. She will be safe with me." Jeremy indicates for me to go ahead of him.

"Just a minute." My father's voice booms around the kitchen.

Embarrassed at the attention I now have on me, I feel my cheeks heat. This is not going to be good.

Jeremy's hand on my back trembles. He subtly lets out a sigh when his father appears.

"Are you insinuating our son cannot be trusted?" Mr. Tyson growls.

"Not at all, but I don't think they should be alone together unchaperoned."

Oh heck!

I want to speak out and so does Jeremy, but we both stay silent.

"Tomorrow evening, Jeremy may walk with Addison. He can collect her at seven sharp."

"Agreed."

"Now is more convenient," I blurt as heat burns my cheeks.

My father narrows his eyes. "I will accompany you home." He grabs my arm and yanks me toward him. "Tomorrow, Jeremy Tyson."

I don't glance back because I'm afraid I'll see Jeremy's sorrow.

My arm throbs as I'm pulled from the church. The

verbal abuse starts the moment we close the car doors.

Tears fall from my eyes and my heart shatters at the disappointment Carter will feel when I let him down. Again.

6

CARTER

WE'RE ALL PLAYING LIKE A BUNCH OF PUSSIES, AND I'M not sure what bug is up Ivan's ass. He's in one hell of a mood and dangerous to be near whether we're his teammates or the opponents. He was in good spirits earlier. Well, as good as you get with Ivan.

I glance at him now and quickly duck as a puck sails over my head. Wincing, I accept the pass from Ivan while he blocks the opposition.

I feed the puck to Bennett, who passes it on to Bryson. Bry doesn't have it for long before he slides it to Camden. He gets the puck in the left corner, moving it around the side of the net before sending an awesome pass toward Bennett, who's ready and waiting in front of the goal. Before the puck can reach him, it hits off my skate and glides into the net.

Yes!

I fist pump the air with my stick gripped in my hand. The game has turned, and the fans go wild!

I do love a home game.

Our luck really did change as we are victorious with another win under our belt.

I leave the ice exhausted but exhilarated. I can't wait to celebrate with Addison. I just want to see her. Maybe get to sample her lips and touch her skin.

"Hey, Carter."

I snap my head toward the voice. Lucy.

"Happy to see me?"

I glance down and check myself. Bryson snorts with laughter and smacks me on the back. "You idiot."

"How the fuck should I know what she was talking about? I wasn't paying attention." I grumble, following his sweaty ass into the locker room.

"Your head is in the clouds these days," Bryson mutters, stripping as he goes. "You need to get it out or you are going to get hurt."

He's right, which I will never admit. His head is big enough already.

After dumping my gear and clothes, I stand under

the hot spray and enjoy the relaxing effect it has on me. I'm usually the last one out of the showers because this is the best time to think. My mind can drift away and settle.

The second my thoughts slip to Addison, I leave the shower. No need to let the guys see how horny I am after a few months of no sex. Oh, my hand has gotten a lot of use, but there is nothing like sinking between the thighs of a beautiful woman. Feeling her nipples rub against my chest. Or watching her tits jiggle as she bounces on me, taking my cock deeper.

Turning my back, I shove myself into a pair of slacks and leave my shirt hanging loose.

Addison is gorgeous and has me frustrated, but she is worth the time. However, my thoughts sometimes drift down a lonely road because I'm not sure she's as committed to whatever we have as I am.

Sighing heavily, I'm fully dressed and ready to go. I tug my phone out of the side pocket in my training bag. I smile as I palm it, seeing Addison has texted.

I should have known better than to look forward to time with her. Angry and once again let down, I shove my phone into the bag and leave.

No way am I replying. I'm pissed at the word she used, "sneak." It grates on my damn nerves.

I'm a pathetic bastard, and I've had enough, regardless as to my thoughts moments before. I'm going to join the guys and have a fucking good time.

"Bry," I shout, "wait up. I'm going to celebrate in the past Carter style tonight." I grin, aware it doesn't reach my eyes. Bry knows it too.

He reaches out and places a hand on my arm. "Talk to her before you do something stupid."

My gut reaction is to laugh. I pause instead.

"Addison doesn't want to talk?" Bryson asks.

I shake my head. "What am I doing, Bry?"

He frowns. "I thought you were into her no matter what."

"I was," I say.

I'm done being the one to always be willing and accommodating. Tonight's big disappointment has set it in motion.

Her face floats in front of my vision, as do my thoughts of earlier. I push them away as I locate my phone and shoot her a quick message.

Me: Why can't you make it?

Addison: My father. I can't sneak out tonight.

"I'm tired of sneaking around. I'm a grown ass adult. Even now, she's telling me she can't 'sneak' out tonight. It's irritating me is all."

"Tell her," Ivan suggests with a shrug, and nudges into Bry. "Tell her to grow up and live her life."

"If you like this girl, then I don't think you have a choice. I agree with Ivan," Bryson grumbles.

Time for a heart-to-heart with Addison.

Me: I need you to meet me. The Pond.

Addison: Give me an hour.

7

ADDISON

MY ARM THROBS AFTER MY FATHER DEPOSITED ME IN my apartment. Maureen was surprised by the abrupt manner.

My heart is breaking because of Carter. I so wanted to be with him tonight. I honestly didn't like the tone of his last message and a very bad feeling settles in my belly.

I slip into my bedroom relieved the lock hasn't been removed. It's the third one in as many days. My father keeps removing them. I keep replacing them.

My father's excuse is because Maureen may need assistance. She is more than able even in a wheelchair, which the specialist has now said could be temporary.

I no longer consider Maureen a friend. She has

been dreadfully mean and bullying toward me. I tried to understand her frustration but no more. She is not a nice person.

No doubt Maureen has called my father about the new lock. So I expect him to come back down soon to remove it. Only this time I plan on refusing him entry. I have not stood up to my father before and it is about time I did. My parents forced me into this situation, so they can accept my privacy too.

I'm currently playing Beethoven loudly in my room to drown out Maureen's voice. She's not as helpless as our parents think.

The music is annoying me, but it's a small price to pay for alone time.

A thud against the door jerks my attention toward it and I curse none to politely.

Another shudder works through the door, and I frown wondering what is going on.

Dashing across the room, I turn the music off. "What are you doing?"

"Get away from the door," my father shouts, his voice full of anger.

I don't have time to move before an axe splinters the middle of the door.

"What!"

More of the door falls away as I rush to hide in the bathroom and engage the locks.

My hands shake as I slowly back toward the small window.

My back hits the wall and I slide down. Tears fall from my eyes, and I cry. I honestly don't know what to do anymore. Maybe, I should have said yes when Carter asked me to move in with him.

I'd thought about it long and hard before I said no. He had looked hopeful. But I hadn't wanted to see disappointment on my parents' faces. I wanted their approval, which I now know I will never get.

"Open this door, Addison," my father yells, rattling the door handle. "I'm sure you would like privacy in the bathroom."

My eyes shoot up to my hairline at his suggestion. With tears streaming down my face, I wrench the dear open. My father stands there with the axe over his shoulder. Maureen is a foot behind him in the wheelchair, a gloating smirk on her hateful face.

"Why?" I ask, my eyes on the shattered door.

"Because you keep applying locks. So removing the door is the cheaper option. You cannot help Maureen if you cannot hear her or won't let her in your room."

"My room is private. I am not Maureen's nurse. If she wants that, she should have stayed home."

My father growls. "We brought you up to be giving, not selfish." He tries to control his temper, and adds, "I can just as easily cancel your walk with Jeremy if you act out again."

"I am an adult," I snap.

Maureen gasps and my father goes red in the face.

"Do not cross me. You will not like the consequences. You understand, daughter?"

I nod.

In my mind I tell him to go to hell.

He stares at me with loathing, expecting an apology from my lips. He will not get one from me today.

"I will ask the young boys to come in and remove the wood." He turns and leaves.

Maureen, who has watched in silence the whole time with a smirk across her lips, stays put. I want to slap her across the face. I know if she doesn't leave, I will.

Clenching my hands, I step forward and grip the handles on the wheelchair.

"I'm not going anywhere." She tries to stop me from moving her.

"You are not welcome in my bedroom. We are no longer friends. I am done." I kick the wood away and then push her into the small living room. I turn my back and return to my room.

I grab the backpack I use for work. In the bathroom, I wiggle free a tile close to the tub and retrieve my savings details. It's an account Carter helped me open. No one in my family is aware of it. I shove it into a shoe and make sure it is hidden at the bottom. I toss in clean underwear, leggings, and tops before pulling the bag closed.

I have no intention of coming home again.

Some people may consider me heartless for leaving Maureen, who is confined to a wheelchair. Maybe I am. But she has full use of everything except her legs, so she can do a lot for herself if she so chooses. She makes out she is helpless when I know she isn't.

I walk straight out the front door without looking back. I immediately flag down a cab to the park.

Carter had been short with me, and I really don't blame him.

Fifteen minutes later, I spot him waiting for me.

I smile, feeling breathless. I always do when I'm with him. By his own admission, I know he was a player before he met me. Even so, I believe him when he says all he wants is me.

He smiles when he sees me, but it doesn't reach his eyes as usual.

I frown. "Is everything okay?" I cup his face.

He takes my hands into his and says, "We need to talk."

My heart drops to my toes. I'm not going to like what he has to say. Inside I feel sick because I was going to ask him if the room he'd offered me is still free. I have nowhere else to go.

I swallow around the lump in my throat and agree.

Dropping my hands, he leads me over to a wooden bench close to the Boston Common Frog Pond.

"I can't stay tonight. I'm meeting some of the team to celebrate our win." He clears his throat. "I want you to think hard tonight about what *you* want, Addison. If it's me, then no more meeting in secret. If you can't do that, then I guess I will see you around. Maybe." He finally turns to look at me.

He'll see the shock I am unable to hide. My tears of despair slowly slipping down my face.

Carter glances once more in my direction and

nervously swallows. "I have to go." He stands. "Message me your answer."

I try and blink away the tears but more fall. I'm not even sure what just happened. In all the time I have spent with Carter, he has never been cold toward me.

You deserve it though.

My conscience doesn't know what it's talking about. No one deserves indifference from the man they love.

And then, it starts to rain.

I tip my face up and let the cold rain fall. I will be soaked to the skin by the time it stops. Either that or I will freeze to death first.

Nothing makes sense. Not anymore.

I've finally left, well, ran away. I'm ready to get on with my life, and he never gave me the chance to tell him that I chose him.

Hours later I can't stop shivering. I haven't moved from the Frog Pond, and I'm not sure my legs will move if I want them to. They feel heavy.

My only choice is to go to Carter's apartment and tell him I have already left my family. Surely, he will be happy and apologize for his attitude earlier. He wasn't the Carter I know.

It's a good walk to his apartment, but I have no choice as I don't have any money.

My muscles ache as I stand, and I deeply inhale. The city looks scary at this time of night. It's something I haven't noticed before because I'm usually with Carter.

8

CARTER

"WHY ARE YOU ON THE WAY TO BECOMING DRUNK?" Camden asks.

"I'm single. I'm allowed to get drunk." I grin, wondering what in the actual fuck I am doing. Not only am I drinking more than I have in a while, but I've been eyeing the girl up for a while. Lucy. The one who I remember having great suction. I'm getting hard just thinking about her mouth around my dick. It's been so fucking long.

Her legs go on for miles and her miniskirt is teasing the fuck out of me. "I haven't had sex in months," I blurt, and wet my lips at the puck bunny shaking her tits at me.

"You touch that"—Camden points—"and you will

have no chance with Addison. Is that what you want? To throw it all away for a quick fuck?"

"I was a dick tonight. I told her it was me or her family. I'm sick of us being a secret. I'm starting to think she's ashamed to be with me." I knock a chaser back, my eyes still on the woman dancing for me.

Camden drops into the vacant chair beside me and shakes his head. "Perhaps you are better off without her if that's how you feel." He frowns into his beer. "You do remember her parents are strict Catholic, right? She'll need a ring on her finger before they let her out of their sight." He snickers. "You'll have to pretend to be a nice Catholic boy."

I snort and shoot him the finger.

Ignoring my friend, I wiggle my finger for the sexy Lucy to come closer. She straddles my thigh, her tiny skirt revealing more leg as she grinds down. My dick is certainly alert at the thought of having a wet pussy massaging it.

I grab her ass and make the mistake of looking down. The wet crotch of her panties is visible. "Fuck!"

"Yes!" She tips forward, and while nibbling and sucking my lobe, she grabs me through my jeans.

It's been too fucking long since I've been touched. I was proving to Addison how serious I was about her. Fool me. If she wanted to be with me, she would have told her parents. She is a grown ass woman.

Seeing the frowns on the faces of my friends, I get angry and guilt washes over me.

"Let's get out of here."

She moans in my ear. "I'm going to give you a night you won't forget." Grabbing my hand, she pulls me out of the bar and straight into a cab.

Her hand dives straight into my jeans, her sure fingers wrapping around my hard flesh. "Oh God," I hiss. "Stop." I pant hard and remove her hand. "Not in the cab." I glance at the driver, who watches through the rearview mirror.

She straddles my lap, and taking my hand, shoves it between her legs.

My dick throbs behind my zipper at the feel of rubbing a hot, wet pussy. I slip a digit beneath the lace and my eyes roll at the wetness I'm gliding through. I can't help myself and slip a finger inside her grasping cunt.

"Oh," she murmurs, fucking herself on my hand.

A loud throat is cleared from the front of the car.

Shit!

I withdraw my finger but not before I tweak the little bundle of nerves that causes her to shiver.

Quickly handing cash over, we stumble from the cab. Her fingers tangle in my T-shirt as she tugs me into the alley. I'm shoved up against the wall, my dick fit for bursting with her hands rubbing and getting my zipper down.

Feels so fucking good having hands other than mine touching my dick. Good just being with someone who wants to touch me.

"Carter?"

My eyes snap open as I face the entrance of the alley just when Lucy wraps a hand around my dick and brings me out to play.

Fuck!

It takes me frozen seconds to snap out of the shock. I shove Lucy away, give her money for a cab, and stride toward Addison wondering how the fuck I'm going to explain this.

She takes off as I call out to her. "Addison? Wait. Let me explain."

Addison stops and glares my way as I get closer. "I don't think there is anything to explain. She had her hands on you. I'm not an idiot." Tears fall down her beautiful face. "You had every intention of fucking her. You'd be at it now if I hadn't interrupted."

Giving me her back, she takes a few steps, stops,

and turns back to me. "Tonight you didn't give me a chance to say anything because I was shocked at the words tumbling out of your mouth. But I'd come to our meeting place to ask if the spare room was still on offer," she cries. "I have everything that means anything to me inside this bag. I'd already chosen you. But I guess between then and now, you chose someone else, huh?"

"Fuck," I curse and reach for her. "I have no excuse for what you saw. As to sex, it wouldn't have gone that far. I promise."

I'd like to think it wouldn't have gone that far; however, I'm not sure about that. Addison doesn't need to know that I doubt myself.

Addison shakes her head. "I don't know whether I believe that or not. You were certainly enjoying her *attention*."

"Please come inside with me and talk," I beg.

With a shake of her head, she says, "I'm not sure that's a good idea."

"Look, I honestly thought I'd fucked up with you earlier. I don't even know why I acted that way and said that crap." I run my hands through my hair. "Afterward, I thought you wouldn't want anything to do with me, so I drowned myself in alcohol."

"And women by the looks of things," she comments, backing further away. "I don't want to talk anymore." With those words uttered, she turns and heads to the crosswalk.

"Wait." I jog to her. "Please don't go like this." I tug at my hair and try to think of a way to make her stay. "I love you," I blurt out.

Her eyes reach her brows as she slowly swallows. "You tell me you love me after I caught you with another woman's hands on your dick? Are you for real?"

I'm fucking this up big time.

"Good night, Carter." Addison crosses the road toward the park, and I do nothing. I stand there like an idiot with no clue how to sort this fucking mess out. I'm under no illusion who's to blame. I'm a fucking idiot.

"You should go after her."

My heart drops. Lucy. I'd forgotten all about her.

"I'm a douche. I'm sorry about earlier. I'm messed up."

"I heard." She sighs. "Do you mind if I come inside and use the facilities?"

I give her a wry look.

"I won't try anything. I honestly just want the restroom at this point. Then I'll call a cab."

Tired and feeling like a bastard, I say, "Yeah, sure." I've already screwed up, so it doesn't really matter.

The doorman smirks as we enter and get on the elevator. Lucy doesn't say anything and disappears into the bathroom.

I move into the front room and pour myself a brandy. I could do with the whole bottle now.

My stomach turns as it firmly sinks into my brain how it must have looked to Addison. The truth is I would have fucked Lucy if Addison hadn't stopped me, and that makes me feel worse. Then I think about how I would have reacted if I'd seen Addison being intimately touched by another guy. I'd have ripped his head off.

Sweet Addison is pure and untouched, and I'm not sure she will ever forgive me.

You didn't fuck Lucy though.

Not sure how long I've been sitting there self-loathing, I hear the click of the front door closing.

A few minutes later, I call security. "Has the woman I came in with left?"

"Yes, Mr. Nelson."

I stagger to bed, strip, and fall on it.

Hopefully, tomorrow I'll forget all about this evening, especially about how much I hurt Addison. I did it so I wouldn't get hurt.

Didn't work out that way.

Sleep won't come as I try to come up with a plan to win her forgiveness...and trust, because I broke that tonight as well.

9

ADDISON

NOT ONLY IS IT COLD BUT IT'S STARTED RAINING, again. I'm soaked to my skin and really don't care anymore. The park bench is lumpy under my butt and legs as I sit opposite Carter's apartment building. I really wish I could get the image of that girl with Carter's penis in her hands out of my head. *Then* he takes her inside with him once he thinks I'm out of sight.

What the hell!

Tears mingle with the rain on my face, but I'm too upset to care. I'm angry and disappointed in him. He told me he could wait until I was ready to go that far with him. That I meant more to him than sex.

What a load of lies.

He had wrongly assumed I would choose my parents and faith over him. Maybe twelve months ago I would have done so. But no more. I'm done with them as I am with Carter.

"Addison?"

Surprised at hearing my name, I lift my gaze and find Carter's friend and teammate Bryson standing over me.

I blink a few times and make out the confusion on his face.

"Why are you sitting in the rain?" He takes my hands and curses. "You're freezing. Let's go inside."

"No!" I tug my hands free. "I'm not going in there. Besides, he has company, and I'm sure she's not there for coffee."

"I'm too late." Bryson runs his hands through his wet hair. "They couldn't have got up to anything yet. Let me go and toss her out."

"They were about to have sex in the alley."

Bryson's eyes pop wide and he curses under his breath. "They didn't?"

"I called out to Carter," I snarl. "She had her hands…" I wave my hand at Bryson's groin. "Ugh! I want to scrub what I saw from my mind, but I'm not sure I will be able to. He was going to do it too!" I glare at Bryson. "If I hadn't come along, they would have done it in the alley. That I do know for sure."

I catch myself as more tears hover. "They're up there now."

"They might be, um, talking," he says.

"Don't be an idiot. You're a guy. Do you take whores up to your apartment to 'talk' to them? I'm not going in there. I don't want to talk to him. I'll find another bench to sleep on." I force myself to stand and glare at the man, sagging before his eyes.

"Look"—he reaches out and takes my hand—"I live in this building too, okay? At least let me get you something dry to put on. I promise I only want to help you. I have a guest room my brother uses when he's in town. Please sleep there tonight so I know you're safe, because I really do not want to sleep outside in this." He smiles.

I hesitate.

"It's much better than a park bench."

I sigh heavily, and say, "Thank you for your kindness. I'd like that."

Bryson slips a hand to my back and guides me across the street.

"He's an asshole for what he's done. He was drinking, but that's no excuse."

"He told me it was time to choose." I sniffle into a torn tissue. "I'd already chosen before I met him tonight. I'd come to ask him if the room he had offered me was still available. I told him that when I interrupted his *good time*. Now I have no money until the bank opens and nowhere to go."

In the elevator, Bryson says, "You do have somewhere to go, Addison. I have the room. And there is no way I'll kick you out."

"Thank you." Breathing deeply, I dry my tears and pull myself together. "I can't believe he did that tonight. Why would he?"

"You have faith, Addie, but Carter doesn't." Opening the door to his apartment, he ushers me inside. "I don't see how he is going to get out of tonight."

"I wish I could scrub it from my mind. But that won't happen anytime soon."

"Here's the bathroom. You need to get in a hot shower. Warm up." Bryson blushes. "Let me get you some sweats and a T-shirt."

I stare at the mirror and a drowned rat stares back. I'm a sight, my tangled hair dripping on to Bryson's floor.

"Please tell me you don't need help?"

I chuckle. "No. I can shower alone."

He smirks. "Good."

"Wait." I reach for him. "Can you not tell anyone, including Carter, that I'm here?"

"You have my word. Besides, Carter deserves to suffer."

Bryson leaves me, closing the door behind him.

SHOWERED AND WARM IN BRYSON'S CLOTHES, I FIND him in the living room with a hot chocolate ready for me.

"How do I find a cheap apartment to rent?" I blow on the drink in my hand. "I up and left and don't really know what to do. I thought I'd be living with Carter."

Bryson kicks his feet onto the coffee table. "Well, now, I hadn't planned on having a roomie, but the bedroom is yours until you know what you want to do."

"You don't mind?"

"No, but you need to be prepared to see Carter. We hang out."

"This is a mess," I moan. "It's all my fault."

"Hell no! Do not say that. This whole mess is Carter's doing." Bryson sounds angry.

"I don't want to get in the middle of your friendship."

He shakes his head. "I was already pissed at him when I saw him leave the bar. Don't worry." He gets to his feet. "I need to get some sleep."

I offer him a wry smile. "Night, Bryson. And thank you." He nods and disappears.

Darkness has never bothered me. Even now as rain lashes at the windows. I'm glad Bryson found me, otherwise I'd be out in that. Letting the sound of raindrops hitting the glass lull me into sleep, I'm jolted awake by a message on my phone.

Carter: Forgive me?

Annoyed, I reply with a definitive no.

Carter: Nothing happened with her.

The nerve of him.

I don't reply.

Carter: Are you still there?

Me: No.

Carter: You're annoyed with me?

Carter: Tonight should not have happened.

Carter: Can I see you tomorrow?

Carter: Addison?

Carter: Please meet me tomorrow. I'm sorry.

Carter: I love you!

Me: Do not lie to me.

Carter: It's the truth. I love you.

Me: How can you say those words after what I saw?

He wouldn't know love if it bit him on the ass.

My phone rings.

I send it to voicemail.

This goes on until I send another message.

Me: I have nothing to say to you other than go fuck yourself.

I go into his contact and block his number. That's it. Tears fall as I switch my phone off and go to the spare bedroom.

10

CARTER

In a foul mood, I've let it out in this morning's training. My head throbs thanks to the alcohol I consumed after my chat with Addison. I feel sick to my gut over what I've done. I can't even explain to myself why I did it. Why the hell did I nearly fuck Lucy? I feel like an even bigger bastard because I would have done a lot of dirty stuff with her if Addison hadn't come along.

Camden tosses his stick in his cubby and faces me. Looks like I won't need to start up anything, he looks ready.

"Did you fuck that girl?"

Clenching my molars, I hiss, "What if I did? It's no one's business."

He shakes his head. "Why did you mess shit up with Addison? She was really into you, and I thought you loved her," he says.

I narrow my eyes and take a step closer to him, pissed because I know I fucked up and I do love her. "You told Molly, didn't you? And she talked to Addison. Fuck!"

"Back off!" He pushes against my shoulder. "And don't blame my wife for your fuckup." He pauses. "I didn't tell Molly about last night."

"Yeah, right!"

"What does it matter whether or not Molly spoke to Addison? She saw you, which you know." Bryson yanks me away from Camden.

"I didn't fuck that girl. I told her that. She interrupted us," I whisper, dropping back on the bench.

"The point you are missing is that you would have done so if Addison hadn't interrupted. Plus, the girl went up to your apartment once Addison left." Bryson raises a brow.

"How do you know she went up to my apartment?" I glare at him. I can hardly breathe, and I want to hurl. "How do you know?"

"Because I came after you. Turns out I was too

late. I found Addison frozen to the bone outside. She's the one who told me about your *guest*."

"I thought she'd left." I pause. "You took her home?"

"Yes."

"I need to talk to her."

"That isn't a good idea. Let her have time. I'm not sure how you are going to get out of it."

I throw my head back and silently agree. My eyes find Camden. "I'm sorry."

Camden nods. "We're good, this time."

I nod, knowing he means never to accuse his wife of anything again.

"What the hell am I going to do?" I put my face into my hands and concentrate on breathing. "I really fucked up, but I swear I never fucked Lucy. She came inside to use the bathroom. That's it. She left."

"Even so, I don't understand what the hell happened with you. You've been all into Addison for a while."

"I don't know what the fuck I was thinking."

"Sex." Theo drops opposite me and shrugs when we look at him. "You needed sex." He clears his throat. "Nearly got it from someone who would give it good. Nothing wrong with that."

"Says the young jock who fucks his way through women," Bennett adds.

"I fuck my way through variety." Theo smirks.

"Asshole," I mutter. "I'm waiting for suggestions as to how to untangle the mess I've made of my life."

"She saw you!" Bryson scoffs. "She's not going to forget that anytime soon. You need to somehow convince her that you didn't do the deed in your apartment." He frowns. "What actually did she see?"

"Enough," I admit.

Wait!

I narrow my eyes. "Why are you being protective of Addison?"

"You didn't see her. I did!" he shouts and walks out.

Fuck!

Pulling myself together, I dress and leave without talking to anyone else.

In my truck, I roll the windows down and let in the cold air. Glancing up, I find Molly rapidly walking toward me. She is all bundled up against the ice.

"Did you fuck that girl?" Molly hisses the words, and it takes me a moment to realize she asked and didn't accuse me.

"No, I didn't." I close my eyes and admit, "I did not fuck her. Not in the alley nor in my apartment." I face Molly. "I love her, Molly. I love Addison, and I royally fucked up."

"Flowers," Molly responds. "Send her flowers. Everyday. Send them. Wait a week and then hand deliver them. When I talk to her, I'll make sure she's aware it wasn't as it seemed." Molly narrows her eyes. "But I'm telling you now, if I find out you lied to me, there will be trouble."

"Yes, ma'am, and I'm not lying."

"You're an idiot, Carter." She reaches through the window and kisses my cheek. "Flowers."

11

ADDISON

AFTER BRYSON TOLD ME TO STAY WITH HIM UNTIL I get myself sorted, I haven't withdrawn any money. It would be pointless having it sitting in my bag for someone to steal.

Yvette here at the library has been kind and, without having been told anything, has made sure I'm not disturbed. I don't usually mind students or even other patrons asking me for assistance. The quiet is allowing me to think on things. Family. Life. Friendships. *Carter.*

Just thinking about him brings tears to my eyes. I really liked him. More than liked, if I'm honest. I'm sad and disappointed. I let my heart lead me toward him and that didn't get me anywhere. Well, except to a broken heart.

I've grown as a person over the last few months, and that's because of him. He's made me see there is more to life than my secluded existence. I should really thank him for that, but I don't quite have that in me. I want to scream at him.

Sighing, I fit the last book back on the shelf and give the rest of the shelf a bit of a dusting. I love working surrounded by books. It's a passion of mine. My parents have never understood why I would want to work in a library. I always describe my job as working in a building of knowledge. There is something for everyone to learn whether that is reading a fiction novel or a factual book.

"Daydreaming?" Yvette whispers.

"Don't you just love this place?" I ask, twirling around to face her.

"That's why I'm still here after thirty-five years." She smiles before it slips into a frown. "I'm a good listener."

"I appreciate that, it's just family stuff." I'm too embarrassed to be honest about what I saw Carter doing last night.

She pats me on the hand. "Well, if you change your mind, you know where to find me."

"Thank you."

"Oh." Yvette pauses and then says over her shoulder, "I actually came back here to tell you Maureen is asking for you."

My heart sinks. "I'll be there in a moment."

What does she want?

Feeling sluggish, I slowly move out from the row I'm hiding behind. Patrons work silently at desks with overhead lights switched on, some on laptops, some leaning over the book they are working from while scrawling in a notebook.

My gaze turns toward the entrance to where Maureen waits. An ache starts to brew across my forehead as I approach. She's all smiles and made-up face. You wouldn't think she has screwed me over more times than I care to remember with my parents for her own gain.

"Why are you here?" I ask in way of greeting. "I'm working."

"Don't you ever get bored in here?" Maureen wheels herself over to a vacant reading nook.

"No, I don't."

"You didn't come home last night."

"And?"

"I haven't told your father, if that's what you want to know."

"I don't care whether you tell them or not. I have no intention of ever going back." I smile, feeling relieved although anxious about what I'm going to do. "I'm free of them, and you."

"Did you move in with *him?*" She sneers, barely containing her disgust.

What to tell her? No way am I going to tell her what I caught Carter doing, nor am I going to admit that I'm currently Bryson Maverick's roommate. "I haven't moved in with Carter." I shrug. "I'm not a helpless female, Maureen. I'm more than capable of taking care of myself."

Her eyes narrow as she tips her head to the side. "I don't believe you."

"I don't care." I offer her a sweet smile, knowing it will rile her up more.

Perhaps I should be playing to her tune so she'll leave. It would be easier, but I'm fed up with constantly having to watch what I say or do. Of always having eyes on me, making sure I don't put a step out of place.

"You know your father will only find you and get

you home, right? It will be easier if you come home when you finish work."

I swallow hard because I know what she's saying is the truth. My father will come looking for me and it won't be pleasant. I cower when my father is angry. Until he grabbed me, he hasn't physically hurt me before. He uses words as punishment. And locked doors.

"Why are you like this? A long time ago we *were* friends, then everything started to change. And now you're in a wheelchair because you were watching me instead of what you were doing. I don't understand you anymore."

Maureen wheels closer and pulls her mouth into a tight line of anger. "You," she hisses, "put me in this chair. You have to pay for that."

I feel more weary than angry now. We've been over this numerous times, but it's always my fault. I do feel guilty, but there is no way I will ever admit to the guilt I carry around. Deep down I know I'm not responsible. I didn't even know she was out that night. It just sits heavily on my chest.

I catch Yvette's eye, and she slightly nods before she's moving toward me. "Addison, dear, I'm sorry to interrupt, but could you help me?"

"I have to get back to work," I say to Maureen. "This is my only warning, stay out of my business." Turning my back on my once friend, I stride behind the counter with Yvette.

"Thank you." I sigh. "I wish everyone would leave me alone."

"Oh!"

My eyes shoot up. "Oh, no! I'm sorry. I didn't mean you." I nod in Maureen's direction. "Maureen and my family."

"Family can be difficult," Yvette says, and clears her throat. "Can you help that young man in the back?" She waves, and he waves back. "He's researching a paper. Old texts. My eyes are bad enough without straining them with the old stuff." Mumbling away to herself, Yvette goes and helps a woman who waits patiently.

I plaster a smile on my face and head toward the man.

Maybe I'll get lucky and he'll be a vampire or something.

Shaking that thought loose, I grin as I reach him.

12

CARTER

IT'S THE SECOND AWAY GAME IN AS MANY NIGHTS AND I'm sick to death of myself. I look in the mirror and see an asshole. It's my own stupid fault, which is like a punch to the gut. What the hell is wrong with me? I love Addison. I told her so, and she laughed in my face. I wince. I could have laid it on her with a bit more finesse instead of telling her after she saw my dick in another woman's hands.

My head hasn't stopped aching since that night a week ago and I can't blame it on alcohol. Wyatt would have me off the team without blinking an eye if I came to the ice drunk. It's the one and only reason why I haven't paid a visit to the liquor store.

I've spent money on flowers that the florist

informs me have been received. But still no word from Addison. I wish she'd at least message me. Oh, wait! She blocked me. How can I get her back if she won't talk to me?

"Coach is glaring." Noah knocks my foot with his stick.

Bryson grunts. "He's going to have you sitting the game out if you don't pay attention." He pauses. "Come on, Carter, you know what he's like."

"You're not the first guy to piss his girlfriend off. Give her time to come around," Theo adds.

"You really think she's going to come around when she caught him about to fuck someone else?" Bryson says, sounding annoyed.

"What've you done to fuck him off?" Bennett stares after Bry.

"I've no idea."

"Stop!" Van yells. "You are men! Stop gossip like women. Yak. Yak. Yak. Stop! *Da!*"

"Molly wouldn't be happy hearing that comment," Camden says under his breath.

Finding humor in my teammates, I shake off the maudlin feeling and get my head out of my ass. We have a game to win, and I won't be helping my team in the direction I was going.

Coach finishes up and we trudge from the board room to the locker room, all of us quiet. The room doesn't smell of body odor at this point, but it will. Sitting on the bench, I lean forward and unzip my gear bag. The first thing I see as I reach inside is my phone with a new text message.

Flowers in Bloom: The girl you are sending flowers to no longer lives at the address you gave me. She hasn't for a week.

Blood rushes through my head and I read the message over a few times. I rub my brow and think. If it's Maureen the florist has been leaving the flowers with, she could be lying. She's told enough of those recently. However, Addison may have moved out. That doesn't sound like her though. She told me she'd chosen me, but I hadn't really believed her. I'd wanted to.

"Fuck, my life!" I curse, tossing my phone into the cubby. I go through the motions of getting ready for the game while my mind is conjuring up different scenarios, none of which make sense. Not from what I know about Addison. She isn't the kind of person to make rash decisions. Something isn't right.

"You're making me nervous with all that jittering you're doing," Sutton hisses.

I give him the finger and continue to pace. He steps in my path.

"Spit it out?"

I open my mouth. Nothing comes out. I try again. "I don't think Addison is living at home anymore. I don't know for sure and it's driving me nuts."

"And you just found out now?" Sutton frowns.

"I've had a florist delivering flowers every day since I fucked it all up. The florist messaged to tell me Addison hasn't lived there for a week. I don't know if it's Maureen lying, or if it's fact. She doesn't know anyone. Where the fuck could she go? What if she needs help?" I feel myself getting worked up the more I speak my thoughts aloud.

A heavy sigh comes from over my shoulder. "I know where she is."

I turn to Bryson. "How?"

"I rescued her from the freezing rain after you fucked up." Bryson runs a hand over his head. "She's...my roommate."

Although a burst of sudden laughter filters into my brain, I see red and lunge for him. I don't get close as Sutton wraps an arm around my waist, yanking me back. "Do not do this."

"He's living with my girl," I snarl.

"You're an idiot." Bryson narrows his eyes. "Would you rather I'd left her on the sidewalk, soaked to the bone, after she witnessed you taking the bunny up to your apartment?"

"It's been a week. You could have told me."

"I promised her I wouldn't. She knows she can stay for as long as she wants." Bry shrugs. "I have zero interest in her in the way you do. She's becoming a friend." He smiles. "It feels like it did when my sister lived with me for a short while. You hurt Addison at a time when she needed you the most." Bryson takes a step back and shakes his head. "It's taken this long for the bruising on her arm to start to fade. Her father didn't like her attitude."

"Enough," Bennett snaps. "Whatever is going on, you need to leave it at the door. We need to win this game tonight, so remember we are a team." My friend and team captain glares. "You got me?"

Exhaling, I nod. "Yes."

Bry holds his hand out.

I hesitate before shaking. "We friends?"

"We always have been." Bry grabs his helmet, gloves, and stick.

I do the same and follow my teammates out of the room. The fans stamp their feet in time to Queen's

"We Will Rock You." It usually fills my heart with exhilaration, today I want to be elsewhere. My teammates know that.

"Carter, looking good!"

The words drift toward me in a voice I recognize. I glance upward and find Lucy hanging over the stand.

I acknowledge her with a tip of my stick before I focus in front of me only to find Bryson scowling.

"Lucy is someone I'm going to talk to before I get back with Addison. I don't want her fucking anything up for me...I will get back with Addison. No way will I give up. I screwed up once in a huge, unforgettable way," I say to no one in particular. "Not again."

Bryson grins.

A lightbulb flicks on in my head. I need an unforgettable way to make it up to Addison.

Grinning, I thump Bryson on the shoulder. "Let's win this fucking game. I've got a girl to get back."

13

ADDISON

"ARE YOU SURE THERE IS NOTHING GOING ON WITH Bryson?" Molly asks, giving me the eye.

I roll mine and shake my head. "He's like a big brother who all the girls are crushing on." I grin. "We went to Whole Foods, and the amount of female attention he got was embarrassing. For me as well as him. I shudder just thinking about it."

The sound of the TV being switched to tonight's game filters into the kitchen. Scarlett being impatient to catch Bennett on screen.

"I've been thinking of talking to Carter. What do you think?" My eyes flicker between Molly and Hailee.

"I'm not a forgiving person." Hailee frowns. "I try to be, but with something like that I'm not sure I could."

Molly gives me a hug and steps away. "Camden tells me he doesn't believe anything other than what you saw actually happened. Carter is a terrible liar. So I'm inclined to believe he didn't have sex with her. Carter probably felt bad that the night the bunny expected didn't happen, so he told her she could freshen up in his apartment." Molly shrugs. "He's broken your trust with what happened, but I don't think your heart is broken just yet."

I shake my head, fighting off tears. "He's sent me flowers every day. Of course, Maureen has taken them in. Jeremy, a man from my family's church, overheard her telling my father. Jeremy and I are friends." I smile. "He's gay and in love with another man. We'd planned to use each other as an excuse to spend time with our partners."

"I haven't seen Carter." Hailee swipes a glass of wine from the counter. "Sutton thinks his friend fucked up but doesn't believe he slept with her."

"The team is coming on to the ice," shouts Scarlett.

Taking our wine and snacks into the living room,

we get comfortable in front of Bryson's huge TV. My eyes immediately find Carter with the large 45 on the back of his jersey. I'm wearing it too.

"I wish it was a home game. We could be there," I mutter, nursing the red wine in my glass. I'm not sure when I drank so much of it, but there's about an inch left.

Scarlett pats my knee. "In two days they have a home game."

"I'll sort passes out," Molly volunteers. She works for Wyatt, so she always takes care of what we need to be at games. No task is too big for Molly.

"I wish I could forget about what I saw."

Molly clears her throat. "If I saw Camden in that position, I'd have taken scissors and cut off his dick." She grins. "Maybe stuffed it down his throat afterward."

"Ew, Molly. That really is an image we don't need." Hailee takes a long gulp of wine.

Scarlett shakes her head. "You wouldn't do that because you love that part of him. You'd tease the ass off him with letting him touch you. Knowing Camden, that would be punishment."

"I've never had sex," I blurt, and look at the

stunned faces of my friends. "I've read enough about it, but I've never had it. Never touched a dick." I smirk. "Well, I might have shaken the hand of one or two in the past."

It takes a moment and then they titter with laughter. "She made a joke!" Molly announces. "I think we need more wine."

"Are you sure about that?" Scarlett laughs. "I think Addison might have had enough."

"Heck no!" I hold my glass out. "I'm just loosening up."

"Oh boy," Hailee mutters under her breath.

Unfortunately, the wine has an opposite effect the more I drink. I was fine until I spotted *that* girl in the stands and then my mood took a turn. The others don't know she's there because I kept it to myself. It hurts though.

The camera doesn't show her again, thank goodness, and now there are two minutes left on the clock. Both teams have played wild and rough with blood being spilled on both sides. Carter's helmet has been tossed to the ice three times, which is why he has a busted lip and what will turn into a black eye.

Then it happens.

Thirty-three seconds left on the clock, and Carter, Bryson, and Ivan throw their helmets down and go for it. Fists fly as more teammates join in. Carter gets yanked off the guy he's fighting by a New York Explorers defenseman. He falls backward over a downed player and *doesn't move*.

The camera focuses on Carter as the team doctor rushes over to him with Wyatt in the lead. The fighting comes to a sudden stop when they realize something else is going on.

Carter still doesn't move.

"Why isn't he moving?" I whisper, feeling all the blood dropping to my toes. "He has to move."

My three friends touch my hands and arm, wherever they can reach to offer comfort.

"Bennett is with him," Scarlett mumbles.

Tears fall when I see the stretcher being brought on to the ice. It's subtle but I catch it. Carter moves his arm.

"Did he get knocked out and he's fine now?" I ask in hope.

My friends can't answer. They know as much as I do, which is nothing.

"I need to go to him." I get unsteadily to my feet.

That's when it sinks in. None of us are in any fit state to drive. I don't have the money to take an UBER. Tears slide down my face and I drop to my knees. Scarlett wraps an arm around my shoulders.

"We'll get an UBER," Molly says. "I'll order it."

"I don't have any money."

Molly shakes her head and fiddles with her phone.

"Does he look okay?" I ask Hailee.

She winces. "I can't see." Taking my hand, she adds, "One of the guys will call soon. They know we're watching with you."

"This can't be happening." I stand and start pacing back and forth in front of the terrace. "We're not together. I shouldn't be seconds from falling apart when we're not together." I get hiccups as the tears flow. "How is this happening?"

Hailee pulls me against her chest. "You love him. He loves you. We all know this." She rubs my back.

"The car will be here in ten minutes," Molly announces.

Scarlett's phone starts blaring through the room. She fumbles it from her pocket.

"Bennett, what happened?"

She listens, her eyes unwavering from mine.

"UBER is on the way. We'll be there as soon as we can. Love you."

"When he fell, his head bounced on the ice. He woke briefly. Looked at Bennett and said your name." Scarlett looks directly at me. "He's unconscious. The team is going to the hospital. I'm to call Bennet when we get there as there will be security at the door."

14

ADDISON

SHORT OF FOUR HOURS LATER, WE ARRIVE AT THE hospital to find chaos. No one knows anything and security is kicking the press outside. Luckily for us, Bennett, Camden, Sutton, and Bryson come outside and take us in.

I'm unnerved and don't know what I'm supposed to do or say. Do I even have any right to ask anything? To be with him? Bryson gives me his strength and stays beside me.

We're sitting huddled to one side of the waiting room while the team becomes restless. They're not the only ones. It's awful waiting to find out what is wrong and why he hasn't woken up.

I blink a few times when *that* girl rushes into the

waiting room. She wildly looks around, and asks, "Is he okay?"

The ones who aren't staring at her look at Bennett for direction.

Bennett clears his throat. "You can't be here."

"I have every right to be here. He's my boyfriend."

"Like fucking hell, he is!" Camden fumes.

My heart sinks to my toes and I want the ground to swallow me whole. I'm worried sick about Carter and desperately want to see him, but there is also a part of me who wants to yell at him for putting me in this position.

A manly throat is cleared in the doorway. All heads turn. A doctor stands tall looking around the room. "This is a hospital with very sick patients, please keep your voices down."

"Sorry, Doctor. Do you have any news on our friend? Carter Nelson?"

The doctor nods. "He's awake and I have his permission to talk to you. Not that there is much to tell. We're keeping him for the minimum two nights. Might be longer. The scans came back okay; however, it would seem he's having an issue with memory."

"When can I see him?" I ask in the silent room. "Please, I need to see he's okay."

The doctor offers me a sympathetic smile. "Soon."

"What kind of memory issue?" Bennett asks.

"Maybe we should discuss this in private." The doctor looks uncomfortable. "He's asking for someone." The doc's eyes flicker between me and *that* girl.

Bennett directs my thoughts. "He woke on the ice, and he told me to tell Addison he loves her. I told him he needed to tell her himself." Bennett takes my hand and pulls me toward the doctor. "Can she see him while we talk?"

The doctor looks extremely uncomfortable now. "That's what we need to discuss."

"I'm not following." Bennett squeezes my hand, facing the doc.

"You really are going to make me say it in front of everyone?"

The doctor's words confuse me as they do Bennett.

"He keeps asking for someone named Lucy," he says.

"That's me." The girl I've come to hate rushes forward and she's out the door before anyone can stop her. The doctor follows and directs her while I stand like a fool next to Bennett. He's saying something to me, but I have no idea what. I can't hear anything with all the blood rushing around in my head. His mouth is kind of blurring with his face and my legs turn to jelly.

"She's going down," someone says, then I'm swung up and lifted against a hard body. "I've got you, sis."

Bryson.

He's the only one who calls me that and has done so for the past two days.

He sits down with me on his lap, tucking my face into the crook of his neck. "What the fuck is going on?"

"I don't know," Bennett answers. "I'm going to find out though."

I watch from beneath my eyelids as Bennett places a deep kiss on Scarlett, takes her hand, and they leave, heading toward where the doctor vanished.

"The big lug did mention he wanted to talk to Lucy before he got you back. The girl has a habit of lying and he didn't want her fucking anything up between the two of you." Bry winces. "He did that all on this own."

"That doesn't make it better." I cry into Bry's shoulder.

"Before he even knew you existed, he did fuck Lucy. Once. That was months before he met you. I promise. She's been hanging around more, but he hasn't taken her on."

"I wish I'd never come here."

Bryson chuckles. "No, you don't. I know you love him. I heard him tell Bennett he loves you. Don't give up on him. None of us know why he asked for Lucy. You could be reading something into it that isn't there."

"You're living in cuckoo land, Bryson."

Bennett and Scarlett come back into the room and I'm sure all color has drained from Bennett's face. Scarlett won't meet my gaze.

Over my head, Bryson and Bennett exchange looks before Bennett moves closer and crouches in front of us. "He's lost eight months. The doctor says he *might* get them back. The doc just doesn't know when." He winces. "For some fucked-up reason, he believes he's been dating Lucy."

My eyes shoot upward.

"He has never dated her, Addison." Bennett grips my hand. "I promise you that. I have no idea where his fucked-up head is at with that. However, Lucy is living it up and refuses to say otherwise."

"What?" Molly hisses. "That whore is not going to be allowed to get her claws into our man."

"Whose man?" Camden queries.

Molly rolls her eyes. "He's ours, Camden. You know what I mean. If you won't tell him the truth, then I will."

"It's not that simple. Don't you think Scarlett and I wanted to blurt the truth out. Seeing that woman hovering around him made me want to punch out the fucking window. We must keep him calm. Zero stress. The doctor is aware Carter is confused and remembering things wrong. He said it could cause undue stress if we tell him the truth. I don't like it. In fact, I'm furious, and when he has his memory back, I'm going to make sure that girl is banned from the arena."

I slowly nod. "I think I want to go home."

"I'll take you," Bryson says, then winces. "Let me sort out a ride, then I'll take you."

I turn toward him and stay hidden while he does just that.

15

CARTER

MY HEAD HURTS MORE NOW THAN IT DID WHEN I FIRST woke. Lucy won't stop chatting and fluffing her hair. It makes me wonder why I'm dating her. I don't date, so why did I change my mind about her? I can't get the information to make sense in my head and it's driving me crazy.

The hospital is sterile and smells of antiseptic and cleaning products. I guess that's better than smelling anything else.

Bennett was in here not too long ago and he gave me such a look that I can't get it out of my head. I know my memory is on the blink, but I don't recall him looking at me in that way before. He looked angry.

Lucy knows what is going on but refuses to tell me. Apparently, the doctor has instructed everyone to let me remember on my own.

Sighing, I glance at Lucy, who is typing away on her phone. It's been in her hand all morning. I don't know what the hell she is yapping about. It's boring as fuck in here.

I scoot up the bed and find Lucy hovering over me. "I can help with that. Let me sort your pillows out."

"I thought you were busy." I nod toward her phone.

"Oh, that. I'm chatting with friends." She smiles.

I must stare too long because I find her weird looking lips moving closer toward mine. I turn my head at the last minute and her lips land on my cheek.

"I'm taking a nap."

"You'll be less grumpy when we're home." She smiles while I try not to react to her words.

"We, um, live together?" I must know.

"Of course, we do, silly."

God, help me!

Why the fuck can't I remember? I do remember waking up in here asking for her, and I guess I got what I asked for. I have this vague memory—like a thin thread—trying to get through to me, telling me I only wanted to say something to her.

"You get some sleep while I go and get something to eat. I'm starving." After collecting her purse, she gives me a peck on the cheek and saunters out.

I need my phone.

Something isn't right, and if Lucy won't tell me what the hell is wrong, then I'll talk to Bennett. Or maybe Camden. Camden can be a fool, but he won't lie about what's going on.

"Mr. Nelson?" The stern voice puts the sense of fear into me as I focus on the nurse standing in the doorway. "What are you doing?"

I sag against the pillow, thanking God it's not Mrs. Clarke, my fifth-grade science teacher. She put the fear of God into everyone who crossed her path.

"You look like you've seen a ghost." The nurse enters the room. "What were you doing hanging out of the bed?"

"Looking for my phone. I need to call Bennett."

"Bennett Johnson. He left his number scrawled beside the phone on your other side. He was very insistent you have access to a phone."

Yes!

"When can I get out of here?" I eye the phone, my attention no longer on the nurse.

"When the doctor says so."

Cursing under my breath, I face the nurse. "The doc said my scans show everything as it should be, right? So I don't need to stay."

"Doctor Scott is concerned because of the amnesia."

"I'm fine."

"Yes, you are," says Lucy, breezing back into the room.

"Hmm," the nurse mutters. "I can see why you're in a rush to get home, but there will be none of that. No strenuous exercise allowed for a month." She grins and leaves the room.

"I hope you don't mind me eating with you. I didn't want you to be alone." Lucy sits and starts picking at a salad.

My eyes stray toward the phone. One moment of peace would be fine. I can't even have that with Lucy hovering.

Whatever!

I reach for the phone and watch as Lucy pauses mid-chew. She swallows hard. "Do you think it's wise using that?"

"It's a phone. I do remember how to use one." I grab the paper Bennett left and quickly dial his number. He answers on the second ring.

"How's the head?"

"The head is just fine," I growl. "If you like me at all, you better come and get me out of here."

He replies, "I'm in Boston. You're in New York. The doc said you had to stay a day or two."

"I'm going crazy here."

"Well, you're in the right place for crazy."

I grind my molars. "Stop being a dick and get me the fuck out of this hospital."

"Give me that phone." I hear in the background.

"Carter, it's Scarlett. How are you feeling?"

"Frustrated," I snap. "Sorry. I didn't mean to snap at you. Will you tell that asshole you are married to, to come and break me out of this place?"

She snickers. "He's already grabbing his keys. It will take four hours or so to get there, Carter."

"Thank you." I sigh in relief. "At least I'm not stuck in LA."

She chuckles. "Is...*Lucy* still there?" I frown at the tentative way Scarlett asks.

"That would be yes."

"Oh!"

I don't like the sound of that. My eyes land on Lucy, who looks entirely too engrossed in my conversation.

"I'll talk to you when I get back, okay?" I say to Scarlett.

"I look forward to it."

"I feel like I've forgotten something important." I eye Lucy. "You wouldn't happen to know what that is, would you?"

"Um, maybe our engagement." She grins while my eyes bug out of my head.

"You're not serious?"

"I wouldn't lie about a thing like that." I can't decide if she's lying or not, but she does look genuinely hurt at my callous remark.

"I can't remember." I wince. "I wish I could."

Lucy throws her trash away and stands beside the bed.

I take her hand and give it a gentle squeeze. "I'm sorry."

"It's okay. I know you don't remember. I'm just glad you remembered me."

Lucy is pretty with long blond hair, natural too. Her smile reminds me of the night we spent together. The way those red lips had wrapped around my dick and sucked me dry.

Do not think of getting a blow job!

"So, um, as I can't remember the last eight months or so, why don't you fill me in?"

Her hand slips from mine and she sits. "I'm not supposed to tell you anything."

"You told me we're engaged," I say, glancing at her ring finger.

"Oh, that was new, and it slipped out."

"How new?"

"Two days new."

"And I didn't have a ring for you?"

"You did. It needed to be made smaller." She smiles. "We collect it next week."

"Okay." I'm still not convinced I'm engaged to this woman. Surely something about her would ring more bells. Why can I only remember that one night of sex? That's all I'd been after, and she'd agreed at the time. What the hell happened between then and now?

"Did I hear that Bennett is on the way to pick us up?"

"Yes." I pause. "Why didn't I ask you for a ride home if we live together?"

"I don't drive." She shrugs. "I figured you'd get one of the guys to pick us up."

I let my eyes drift closed to shut her out; I need to sleep and remember.

16

ADDISON

"Are you sure about this?" I gawk at myself in the mirror.

"You look hot." Bryson grins from over my shoulder.

The girls thought it a wonderful idea to change my wardrobe from sensible to glued on. I don't think I've ever been as uncomfortable. "Guys are pigs," I mutter.

Bryson's eyes snap to mine and a slow grin appears on his face. "You have gorgeous legs." He backs away. "Besides, women are just the same as guys. You saw in Whole Foods how those women eyed me up. It gets uncomfortable and I don't like it." He sighs. "I have to remind myself to play nice in the public eye because the one time I don't could end my career. It's just how it is regardless of how fair a boss Wyatt is."

Bryson turns me around so that I'm facing him. "The only way to make him remember is to have you constantly in sight. When he does remember, he's going to be pissed at that woman."

"Why would she do something like this? Surely she knows he'll remember."

"Forget about her." Bryson takes my hand and gently tugs me from the restrooms. "I'm going to show you off by the rink." He wiggles his brows. "Between me and the others, we'll make sure he gets to see you."

I eye him warily. "Why does the sound of that make me nervous."

He shakes his head and ignores my comment. We walk down the hallway toward the elevator. Once inside, he says, "Carter can't play for another few weeks. He's frustrated as hell about that. But he'll be there watching." He pauses. "Make him look at you, Addison. Wiggle your, um, assets in his face."

"I'm not wiggling my boobs in anyone's face." I huff and curse under my breath.

This whole plan makes me nervous. Molly and the

others think it's a wonderful idea. I don't mind the new clothes because they're nice, my confidence needs to grow a bit is all. The idea is to keep me in Carter's sight so that his memory of me will come back.

If what Carter told me is the truth and what he told his friends, then I can do this. I feel sick when I think of him with her. What have they been up to if he thinks she's his girlfriend? That's what worries me. I keep telling myself it doesn't matter because once he gets his memory back, I'll be his again. But it does matter. I love him. He said he loves me. *Lucy* needs knocking into next week for what she is doing to him, and me.

"Stop fidgeting," says Bryson, taking my hand and leading me toward the ice. He groans. "She's with him. *Fuck* that girl!"

"I don't think—"

"Exactly. Don't think. Do." Bryson releases my hand and puts an arm around my shoulders. "Just play along."

"Why do those words make me nervous?"

He chuckles. "Nothing to be nervous about, babe."

I'm marched over to Carter and *her*. The only

consolation right now is that Carter looks annoyed with the woman beside him.

Bryson says, "Carter, can you look after my girl while I practice? Her name's Addison." He kisses me on the cheek and shoves me beside Carter.

"We haven't met, I'm Carter Nelson." He smiles and I don't miss the way his eyes travel over my face, a frown forming on his. "Have we met before?"

I swallow hard and search over his face before I hold his gaze. My cheeks heat from the way he's looking at me.

"Hey," Lucy growls. "Leave my fiancé alone?"

Carter winces and I find I must blink a few times so the tears don't fall. I glance away and search for Bryson, who is chatting away with Ivan while Coach is about to lose his temper as he watches them.

Carter and Lucy whisper beside me, words that I don't catch. I do recognize Carter's pissed off tone. I've been in his presence when he's used it once or twice before.

Unable to sit here and pretend everything is okay, I quickly get to my feet and leave the ice. This whole thing of me throwing myself at Carter is not going to work. At least not with his *fiancée* present. When the hell did that happen?

Blinded by tears, I make my way toward the back of the building. There is a loading dock with a fantastic view of the city.

I dodge around people but come to a stop when someone reaches out and takes my wrist. "Addison?"

Lifting my gaze, I'm relieved to find Riley. She shoos Ethan toward the ice and gently takes me to one side, shoving a tissue into my hand. "It's not going well, huh?"

"He's engaged to her," I wail as I try to bring my emotions into check.

Riley's eyes pop wide. "No way will that happen. Ethan is under the impression Carter is irritated with her. Carter knows something is wrong but can't work out what. Trust me. Not one of the guys will let him marry her. They're not even sleeping in the same room."

Blinking through my tears, I ask, "They're not? How do you know?"

"Because Ethan told me she was asleep in the spare room when he took Carter some protein powder." Riley shrugs. "Carter may have lost his memory, but he isn't stupid."

I snort.

Riley grins and slides her arm through mine,

tugging me back toward the rink. "The man will see how much we all love you, and how much we dislike Lucy. He'll work it out."

"I wish I had your confidence."

"What happened?" Bryson asks, opening the door as we push it, and we nearly fall into him. "Where'd you go?"

Riley clears her throat. "Apparently, they're engaged."

Bryson looks confused, and asks, "Engaged in what?"

I stare at him until his eyes shoot up to his hairline. "Fuck me! For real?"

"That's what she said, and he didn't say otherwise," I say.

"Well, she's disappeared. So now is your opportunity." Bryson squeezes my hand.

Carter moves toward us, his eyes fixed on mine. As he moves past us, he snags my hand with his and takes me with him. My heart flips as I stumble along. I glance back over my shoulder and get a thumbs up from Bryson and Riley.

The moment we're alone in the hallway, Carter releases his hold and starts to pace. "Why are you familiar to me?"

"When did you get engaged?" I counter because I'm more annoyed and upset than I want to admit to myself.

He runs his fingers through his hair. "I have no idea." He pauses. "We know each other?" He gives me a penetrating stare so there is no mistake he's now referring to me. "I remember Lucy, but nothing since I was with her." He winces. "Yet, you feel familiar to me. Like home. It makes no sense. It's frustrating not knowing how my life has been over the past eight months." He moves closer and I back into the wall. He follows me, crowding into my space.

I reach out and touch his sides, he shudders in response. "You arouse me," he blurts out. "But I'm with someone who doesn't. I don't understand." He's clearly confused.

I swallow down the words I want to say, and slip from his reach. "You have to remember on your own, Carter. No one can tell you."

I give him one last look, no doubt he'll be able to see the longing on my face, but I force myself to put one foot in front of the other. I desperately want to turn around and run into his arms. Tell him everything.

I don't.

17

CARTER

THE SECOND I'M BACK IN THE ARENA, I SEARCH OUT Bryson, who luckily is close. I don't greet him. "Addison, is she really your girlfriend?"

He narrows his eyes and folds his arms across his chest.

"Carter, what's going on?" Lucy asks.

"Bry?"

"My sister," he says. "You'll know the"—his eyes land on Lucy—"truth when you get your memory back."

I open my mouth to respond, but snap it shut. "Why do I feel like everyone is in on something that I'm not?"

"Don't be silly." Lucy takes my arm. "Maybe we need to go home."

"Yeah, Lucy," Camden hisses, "why don't you go back to *your* home."

No clue what is going on has me close to losing my temper. "Watch your tone with her."

My friends look startled at my reply, but I figure we're done here.

I glance at Lucy and realize she's delighted that I defended her. Isn't that what boyfriends are supposed to do?

Feeling more confused than ever, I take Lucy's hand and we leave the rink.

Outside in the cold, my eyes land on the sweat girl who Bryson had introduced. Addison. She'd taken my breath away and I know in my lost memories is where Addison lives. But why and how do I know this? What is it about her that feels more real than the woman whose hand I currently hold?

Alone in the hallway, I'd felt my body stir and pleasure at being with her. She'd looked sad. Upset even when Lucy had called me her fiancé.

"It's cold, Carter. We need to leave." Lucy tugs on my hand and I reluctantly follow her toward my truck. She'd wanted to drive the beast, but no way in hell was that happening.

I set the heat blasting and turn to Lucy. "Are we really engaged?"

Surprised, she stutters, "Yes! Why would you doubt that?"

"Because none of my friends knew about it. I'm sure I'd have mentioned it to at least one of them if I'd planned on popping the big question. They didn't know." I rub my brow.

"It was all new is why. Don't read too much into it." Lucy clips her belt in place. "I'm ready for lunch."

As I'm driving out of the lot, I notice Addison with her coat pulled up around her ears, walking toward the exit. Doesn't she have a ride?

Instinct has me slowing and winding the window down. "Addison, let me give you a ride?"

She hesitates. "I'll walk."

"It's freezing. Please let me drive you wherever you're going." Maybe she thinks I'm alone and it makes her nervous. "Lucy is with me." I smile. "Please get out of the cold."

"Honestly, Carter," Lucy hisses. "The girl obviously wants to walk."

Addison, having overheard, grins. "I'd love a ride. Thank you." She clambers into the back.

I turn to look at her and don't miss the evil glare passing between Addison and Lucy. There is so much going on in here. I clear my throat. "So, Addison, where are you heading?"

"Home."

"And that is?"

She grins. "Same building as you."

Lucy hisses, but one glare at her from me shuts her up.

I start driving, wondering what is going on with this girl. I know her. It's obvious. I curse my stupid memory loss. I want to remember Addison. Even her name sounds hot. I keep glancing at her through the rearview mirror, and when I do, I find her eyes on mine.

I'm more heated than usual as I pull into the parking garage beneath the building. I hold the door for her to get out and notice a lovely blush on her cheeks. She won't meet my eyes as I follow her toward the elevator.

She glances behind me. "Aren't you forgetting someone?"

"What?" *Oh fuck!*

I turn back and see Lucy still sitting in the truck. I shrug and watch her climb out when she realizes I'm not helping. I'm not usually bad mannered, but with her, nothing feels right. Not like it does when I look at Addison.

"What is wrong with you?" Lucy curses, storming toward me, um, not me, Addison. She jabs Addison in the chest, which causes her to take a surprised step back.

I grab Lucy's wrist and tug her away. "Don't you lay another finger on her," I growl. "What the hell is wrong with you?"

"Me?" she screeches. "You opened the door for her, and left me, your fiancée, in the car."

"Are you for real, right now? Addison was on my side. You weren't. I'm sure you know how to open a car door. I'm not your servant." I make sure to keep my body between Lucy and Addison as we get on the elevator.

It's a silent ride up until Addison leaves. The moment the doors close, I turn on Lucy. "How could you attack someone?"

"She was all over you in front of me!"

"Get over yourself, Lucy."

I'm sure she wants to say a lot more than she does

as she snaps her mouth closed. I'm furious with her, so when we're inside the apartment, I head straight for my bedroom and close and lock the door.

She tries the knob and I smile to myself that I've finally gotten the balls to keep her out of my space. Surely if I loved the woman enough to ask her to marry me, I wouldn't be relieved she's out of sight.

A headache brews in my temple as I strip and head for the shower.

I wish there was a pill or something that would give me my memory back.

18

ADDISON

THIS IS A BAD IDEA. A VERY BAD IDEA.

I mutter to myself as I walk into the building I used to call home. I grew up here. My father taught me to ride a red bicycle on the sidewalk outside. As a child everything seemed perfect. I had two parents who loved me. A nice home. Food always on the table. And then I grew up and everything changed, including my parents.

Even Maureen was different back then, she certainly wasn't bitter and vindictive. She'd gotten worse over the years, just like my father had.

My legs tremble as I slowly walk up the stairs toward my parents' apartment. It's not something I want to do, but it's something I feel I should. I really don't want any ill will between us. If I'm honest with myself, I'm scared to death of facing my father. I need to though. I need to get it over with so I'm not constantly looking over my shoulder wondering when he's going to show up. Because he will. That I know with certainty.

Once upon a time, I thought my life was going in a different direction, and now, now I feel adrift with no direction. It leaves me feeling very uncertain about my future. I honestly don't know what I would have done without Bryson. He's so much more than a player.

He isn't even that, I think to myself as I approach the landing of the fourth floor. Bryson wants others to think he's a player when in fact, he isn't. He's a good guy and someone who listens when he's spoken to. Telling him I think he's sweet had surprised him and he'd blushed.

I'm not going to find anything sweet behind this door, I think as I knock.

My heart beats rapidly behind my breastbone as I hear footsteps on the hardwood flooring in the hallway of the apartment. It's my mother approaching. My father's footsteps are a lot heavier.

The door starts to open. I quickly wipe my sweaty

palms down my jeans. I overhear hushed voices and then I'm facing the woman who gave me life. My first instinct is to rush into her arms, but there is no welcome on her face. Her mouth twists into a tight line of displeasure.

"You shouldn't be here." She opens the door wider and indicates for me to enter.

"You're still my parents," I whisper, stepping past her.

Muttering all the way into the kitchen, my mom sets about making tea. She's always been a tea drinker, whereas I've always pretended to like it. I will again today.

Clearing my throat, I say, "I'm not here to cause trouble. I just don't want us arguing. You're my parents."

"But yet you ran away from home?" My father surprises me. I didn't know he was here because my mother answered the door.

"You scared me." I swallow around the fear in my throat. "I got fed up with not having my own life. It's mine to live."

"We did not bring you up to live with a man out of wedlock," my father hisses. "It is wrong and against everything you have been taught."

"I'm not living with a man out of wedlock."

Their eyes snap to my left hand. If I wasn't scared, I'd roll my eyes at the assumption. "We're not married...*and* I am not living with him. I'm sharing an apartment with someone. Bryanna," I lie. I'm going to hell.

"Maureen told us you were living in sin with that man." My mother sits at the table with me. "You are not?"

I sigh. "No, Mother. I left for myself. Not for anyone else. I'm not Maureen's keeper. The accident happened because she was spying on me. That was not my fault, and you need to stop blaming me. You are *my* parents and should support *me*."

My father's eyes light up. "You have some backbone at last!"

I glare and he laughs. "Maureen said it was your fault she was hit by a car. You said nothing, so we assumed she spoke the truth." He sighs and stares at my mother, having a silent discussion, then he continues, "I am sorry I hurt you the other night. I did not mean to do that." He nods. "We will forgive you. So you can come home now."

"I'm not coming back here." I stand and edge toward the door, my head telling me this conversation is about to go south. "I can't live under your rules anymore. I have a new home and I like it."

My father growls and sends a chair flying as he charges toward me. I quickly fumble with the door. I manage to get out of the apartment and down the hallway. My feet are going faster than my body as I fall and stumble downstairs, the bannister the only thing stopping me from falling the rest of the way.

At the bottom I fly out of the building and straight into Bryson's arms. He grabs me to him as my father flies out after me.

Seeing me in Bryson's arms with his muscles and tattoos on display stops him cold.

"What the fuck," Bryson whispers.

Clinging to Bryson as a lifeline, I say, "Dad, I want you to meet Bry*anna*."

He gets so mad but puts a lid on it when two cops pull up. They're not here for us, but they cast a look our way.

"Please take me home."

Bryson squeezes me tight. "Of course."

I'm so glad Bryson talked his way into coming with me. Then again, Bryson saw the bruising on my arm from before.

"He's a piece of work." He gives me a look. "Please do not go near him again."

"I won't. I had to try."

He nods. "Yeah, I know."

"Has Bennett called about Carter? Is he okay?"

"I want to say yes, but the truth is he isn't okay."

19

CARTER

"Theo," I growl, "this shit is not funny."

"Okay." He snorts with more laughter.

"Why is my life making everyone amused? What have I done in my past life to deserve this shit?" I grumble.

"You do realize if you hadn't knocked yourself out, then you wouldn't be in this shit?" Theo counters, and snaps his mouth closed.

I narrow my gaze. "So none of this would be happening if I hadn't knocked myself out, huh? Which means this circus is all new? To me and you guys?"

Theo, for once, refrains himself. So I direct my gaze Camden's way. "I've known you longer. Talk."

I throw up my arms, annoyed. "I know what the docs said, and I don't believe that. Just tell me one thing. Was I really dating Lucy?"

I glance between my friends and finally Camden clears his throat. "I'm going to be in trouble for this, but I refuse to lie." He clears his throat again. "No, you were most certainly not."

Incredulous. What assholes! "You are my friends and you let me believe I was dating *that*?" I point toward the living room. "I can't believe it."

Camden winces and Theo laughs.

"At least you didn't fuck her." Theo smirks. "She has a great ass though."

"That is not funny," I snap. "You two got me into this mess, so you can help get me out of it."

"Hey now." Theo bristles. "I had nothing to do with you fucking her. This mess is yours and yours alone, my friend."

Wanting to argue, I force myself to keep my mouth shut on the topic. "Just help me get her and her friends out of my fucking space." I calm. "Please."

Theo rolls his eyes and smacks me on the shoulder. "Why didn't you say so?" He strolls out into the chaos.

I glance at a somber looking Camden, who shakes

his head. "I shouldn't have gone along with it. We thought you'd remember the day after. You didn't. We didn't know what to tell you. For what it's worth, I'm sorry."

I squeeze his shoulder. "It's not your fault. You all did what the doctor told you to do." I shrug. "Let's end this and then you can tell me everything I've forgotten. Including why I can't get Addison out of my head."

Camden stutters, which is new for him as we both walk into the living area.

This is not going to be fun.

"Sorry, ladies, but the fun's over. Everyone out," Theo announces with glee.

Lucy looks to me. "Carter, honey. You said I could have friends around."

"I want you out as well, Lucy. I don't like liars."

Lucy glares at Camden before smiling at me.

I snap, "Do not try anything. I remember, Lucy. I remember how we only fucked that one time. I haven't fucked you since, and we are most certainly not engaged," I shout. "Now get out. All of you before I call the cops."

At my words, they start scrambling to collect their stuff, which is spread all over the damn place.

Camden, Theo, and I stand against the wall watching over them to make sure they don't take anything of mine. It's also intimidating them. I'm pissed as hell that she would pretend something like this. I'm pissed at my friends too, but I'll eventually get over that.

The second they're out the door, I grab my phone and block Lucy's calls, then I delete her contact info.

"So." I turn and face my two friends.

Theo cringes and heads toward the door. "I have something to do. See you at practice." He's gone.

Camden gives Theo the finger before he releases a tired sigh. "If you end up with a monster of a headache, it's your fault."

I nod and move around the kitchen making us coffee. Once in hand, we sit in the living room. "Tell me everything, please. No pussyfooting around."

"I will." Camden swallows and starts talking.

When he's finished, we sit in silence while I soak in what he's told me. I trust it to be true even though I have no recollection. "I knew she felt familiar," I whisper. "I fucked it up though, right?"

Wincing, Camden nods. "She was there at the hospital. She was heartbroken when the doctor said you were asking for Lucy, which tells me you still have a chance with her." He smiles. "Why else do you think she agreed to let Bryson bring her around the ice? She wants you to remember her."

I rub at my jaw, hating the clouds in my head. "I think…" I pause. "I think I need to talk to Addison." I sit there wondering how badly I screwed up. Hearing it from Camden won't be the whole story. "What'd you think?"

"If I argue with Molly, I usually just kiss her into silence." He smirks. "It shuts her up."

I frown. "I can't remember if I've had sex with Addison."

"You haven't."

"How would you know that?"

"She told the girls she's never had sex. Not long after, you knocked yourself out." He shrugs, but I don't miss the amusement in his gaze. "She's waiting for you to get your head out of your ass."

"Wait a minute." I frown. "Why is she hanging out with Bryson?"

"They're friends."

"How friendly?"

Camden laughs. "You can't be jealous of Bryson when you can't remember Addison." He sighs, and adds, "They're roommates. Bryson has no interest in her, and the feeling is mutual. The girl is in love with your sorry ass. *So* I suggest you pull yourself together and get your girl back."

"Do you trust Lucy not to fuck it up?" I ask.

"Hell no!" Camden shudders. "You need to get to Addison before Lucy does." He grins. "Molly will be proud that I remembered everything she told me to tell you."

I pause a moment and laugh. "I should have known Molly was behind your sudden wisdom."

"I love her. She always makes me look intelligent."

Chuckling, I say, "Honestly, you don't give yourself enough credit." I cringe. "That's enough of that shit."

20

ADDISON

THE SECOND BRYSON HITS THE ICE, LUCY HAS ME cornered. I think she deserves the nickname of wicked witch. She'd look at home on a broomstick. Maybe if it were shoved up her—*Stop that thought.*

"Hello, Lucy." I grin.

After talking with Bryson, we agreed it would be best to be polite to the girl. No need to drop to her standards. I won't give up on Carter though. No way will I do that.

"I didn't think I'd see you around here now that Carter and I are getting married." Her false smile and eyelashes need to be wiped off her face.

"I'm with Bryson." I let my eyes drift toward the ice, where the guys are warming up under the watchful eye of Coach Van and Wyatt. "He's hot, don't you think?" I make sure my tone is light and flirty, but little does she know it's Carter who I'm watching closely. "You should see him in only a towel." I face her. "I drool. I mean, who wouldn't?"

Shut up, Addison!

"Don't you think he's hot?"

"He is. I like his tattoos."

Feeling wicked, I add, "You should see the ones he doesn't show in public." I pretend to fan myself. "They're in delicious places."

"Oh," Lucy murmurs, her eyes trailing over the man in question.

Bryson catches us and sends a few wary glances our way before I notice a frown cross his brows. He narrows his eyes and shakes his head, a smirk on his lips.

"He's really into you," Lucy comments.

Bryson isn't into me, but I'm not about to announce that to her. "He is. *Carter* is all yours."

Lucy gives me such a glare I'm surprised she doesn't leave scorch marks on the ground when she stomps away in a huff.

Her words did make a dent in my armor, which is weak at the best of times. I played her well with

Bryson though. I smile as I head in the opposite direction after a glance at the ice. Carter is focused on me, so I offer him a beaming smiling. *Oh yes!* He stumbles before righting himself. Bryson thumps him on the back and together they start horsing around before Coach lets loose with a load of Russian. No doubt cursing them out. I should pay more attention when Coach Van is riled up and maybe I'll learn some words myself.

"Addison?" A shard of pleasure goes down my spine when Carter shouts to me.

I turn and wait for him to catch up. He's taller than I am, but with his skates on, he towers over me. A blush creeps up my cheeks as I take in the sweaty, sexy man before me.

"Will you have dinner with me?" He sounds nervous and full of anxiety as he asks me something he hasn't before. We never went out to dinner. We'd meet for an hour here and there when I could sneak away.

My belly flutters the more I hold his gaze. I lick my lips and his eyes follow, becoming excited.

Clearing my throat, I say, "Lucy reminded me you two are getting married." I try to keep the hurt from my voice, but it seeps in anyway. Bryson and the others have reassured me that Carter hasn't had sex with Lucy since before he met me. It just hurts knowing she's living with him and using him. The other day I felt like hitting Carter over the head myself.

"That is not happening," Carter hisses before clearing his throat. "I kicked her out yesterday. I can't imagine asking Lucy to marry me." He shudders. "I get the feeling you're the one I'm supposed to be close to." He offers me a gentle smile. "Please, have dinner with me?"

"Yes." I don't hesitate now. "I'd really like that."

"I'll pick you up at eight. Is that okay?"

I grin. "I'll be ready. You know I'm Bryson's roommate, right? So you don't have far to go."

"I do." He frowns. "He, um—"

I laugh. "Don't worry. Bryson is like a brother. We're friends." I hesitate, then add, "He's not the man I'm interested in."

"Oh." Carter's gaze finds mine as he moves closer. He reaches out and brushes a tendril of hair from my face, his touch sending tingles of pleasure to certain parts of my body.

I swallow hard and tip my face up. "I'll see you tonight, then?"

"Mmm," he mumbles, and holding my gaze, he dips down and presses a lingering kiss to my cheek. "You will." Very slowly as he pulls away, he trails his fingers from my shoulder to the tips of my fingers. Goose bumps erupt over my skin as I turn and flee into the safety of the women's restroom.

I go straight to the sinks and glare in the mirror above. My cheeks are bright red to look at and they burn. "What on earth is wrong with me?" I turn the faucet on and splash cold water on my face and the pulse points on my wrist. I'm crazy. Carter always made me hot and bothered before, but that out there was something different. That was hopefully the prelude to something so much more.

My eyes shoot up to my hairline. I don't have anything sexy to wear. I have evening wear, but nothing that would get a man hot under his collar.

Molly!

If anyone has anything sexy in her closet, it will be Molly.

I dash from the restroom and smack into the woman herself. I quickly explain what I need.

Molly gives a loud barking laugh. "I have just the thing."

21

CARTER

"THE WHITE SHIRT," THEO SAYS, SHAKING HIS HEAD AT the black I'm currently wearing. I raise a brow, and he looks disgusted with me. "I can't believe you used to be a player when you can't even dress to attract. What's wrong with you?"

Grabbing the shirt at my neck, he tugs it free and tosses it to the bed. "White." He grins. "The chicks love guys in white shirts and black slacks."

About ready to lose my patience, I briefly close my eyes and inhale, then slowly exhale. I should have said no when he told me he was coming to help me out. I'm a guy. We don't do the same stuff women do before a date. Well, I never used to. The asshole even handed me a razor when I said I was going to shower, his eyes glancing below my belt. All it had taken was one dark look to have him tossing it in the trash, his laugh carrying through into the locked bathroom. No way in hell was I putting a razor anywhere near my favorite body part. I shudder at the thought. I may have used scissors. That's my secret.

Smiling to myself, I finish getting the shirt on and find myself admitting that it does look good. The slacks are tailored to fit, so yeah, I'm happy with how I look.

Theo snorts, his eyes full of mirth over his phone, which is clamped in his hands.

"Anyone would think I've never been on a date before," I grumble.

"Have you?" Theo tosses back.

I give him the finger and turn away. "Why are you here again?"

"I'm hanging out with Bry."

"No hot dates?"

"Nope."

I frown and turn back to my friend. "What are you not saying?"

He averts his gaze. "It doesn't matter." Forcing a smile, he wanders out into the living room.

I follow.

"Let's go," he shouts from the hallway.

There is something wrong with me turning up to collect my date with a friend tagging along.

At the elevator, I say, "Can't you hang back five minutes?"

He chuckles. "No way! I want to see your face when you see Addison."

That gives me pause. "Why?"

"Molly is helping her get ready." Theo laughs and pushes the down button before rubbing his hands together. "You look worried."

"I'm afraid I'm going to fuck up. Again."

"You still don't remember her, do you?"

"No."

"Don't worry," Theo says. "Trust your instinct with Addison." He shrugs. "She likes you. So as long as you don't slap anything else into Lucy's hands, you'll be good."

"Ouch!" Theo grabs his shoulder and rubs after the punch I place there.

Bryson is waiting for us at the door and rolls his eyes as he looks us over. "Do I even want to know?"

"No," I growl before clearing my throat. "I've come to collect my date." I grin.

He stumbles into his apartment as the door gets

tugged open behind him, and Addison appears. I practically swallow my tongue at the girl before me. She takes my breath away.

Theo whistles and gets tugged into the apartment as Addison moves toward me. Bryson gives me a warning look and closes the door.

"You look beautiful." I stumble over the words because I can't stop looking at her bare legs. She's wearing lethal looking heels and of course I imagine her sexy long legs wrapped around me, the shoes on her feet digging into my ass.

Clearing my throat, I take her hand and force my gaze above her chest. Her cheeks are rosy and her lips twitch with nerves. "I think we better go."

Once we reach the sidewalk, I take a chance and lead her into an alcove. She frowns, her eyes filling with hesitation as I cup her sweet face. "I need you to know how much I appreciate you giving me another chance." I search her eyes and continue, "I can't take my eyes from you." Reaching for her hand, I place it over my heart. "Can you feel that? It's racing so fast because I'm with you. That's how you make me feel." A wry grin comes over my face. "Like a teenager with his first crush."

The delighted smile she gives me lights up her

whole face. "You have your memory back? I'm happy for you. My trust was broken, Carter, but I love you too much to push you away."

"I do have my memory back," I lie, not wanting her to know I can't remember. I've hurt her enough from what I've been told and need to make up for it. Then I go for the truth. "I promise I'm all yours. I have been since we first met." I drop my forehead to rest gently against hers. "Do you believe me?"

She wraps her arms around my waist. "Yes." Reaching up, she brushes her lips over mine. "You promised me food."

Grinning, I intertwine our fingers and move her along the sidewalk. We only go around the corner to my favorite Italian restaurant. They're always busy and booked well in advance, so I may have gotten the owner two seats at our next home game. Good seats too. A first for me.

The second we step inside, my nose twitches at the Italian spices in the air. Oregano, basil, rosemary, and others I can't name. Addison stops a moment and looks around the popular spot.

"I know you like Italian," I whisper into her ear, making her shiver. I brush her naked shoulder with my lips and smile.

After being embarrassingly gushed over, we're seated in the back of the restaurant, away from prying eyes. My eyes rove over Addison in the black cocktail dress. The neckline dips extremely low, whetting my appetite at the sight of her breasts trying to escape.

She clears her throat, and my eyes lift quickly to hers, which are full of amusement. I grin. "You're gorgeous, Addison. Can't blame me for looking."

"I enjoy having your eyes on me. I feel things." Her cheeks flame and her head dips.

Reaching across the table, I gently take hold of her chin and lift her gaze to mine. "Don't be embarrassed." I give her a wry smile. "I feel things too." I clear my throat. "However, what you make me feel can become embarrassing in public." I wiggle my brows and enjoy the sound of her laughter. She turns a brighter shade of red. "Subject change before you burn this place down."

"Good idea."

22

ADDISON

THE MEAL IS LOVELY AND SO IS THE COMPANY. IT makes me sad to think we've never spent this time together before. It was always an hour here or there. Although, I considered that time special, it was nothing like this evening.

My body feels alive for the first time in my life, and I want nothing more than for the night to never end. Real life always gets in the way. Well, it has in the past, at least for me. I'm still raw over what I caught him doing, and I really am trying to get over it. Trying to trust him again. It isn't easy, but it is what I want because I have strong feelings for him.

Carter approaches my side of the table and holds out a hand. "Let me take you for coffee."

I place my hand into his and pleasure sizzles down my spine. He plays with my fingers, his eyes searching mine. Trying not to become too embarrassed, I step into him and press my lips on his cheek. "Thank you for a lovely dinner," I whisper.

The big man shudders and sharply inhales. "We better leave," he mutters, his voice husky.

I smile, enjoying how he reacts to me. It's thrilling having such a guy become enthralled in little ol' me. I still haven't decided how far I'm wanting to go with him tonight though. I got ready with every intention of trying my hand at seduction after Molly gave me tips. My only hesitation is that I want to stay with him and not just for a night. I'm sure that's what Carter wants, but he hasn't said anything aloud and it's bothering me.

Before everything turned upside down, I thought that was his intention when he asked me to move in with him. I of course messed that up by letting my guilt dictate where I lived. Not anymore though. I must be assertive.

"Such deep thoughts for such a pretty lady," Carter murmurs into my ear.

I tip my face back so I can see his eyes, and ask, "You want me?"

His eyes shoot wide as a sexy smirk appears on his lips. "I always have." He clears his throat and stops walking. He cups my face in his large hands. "Listen to me, Addison. Yes, I want you. I want you with every breath I take. But not until you're ready to go the next step with me." He pauses. "You are my girl-friend. I never stopped thinking of you as that when I fucked it all up." He takes a step away. "I don't know how to make you believe that's it's you I want to be with."

Sighing in relief, I throw myself into his arms and hold on tight. "I believe you, Carter." I nuzzle into his neck and feel his response much lower. I smile and add, "I'm relieved you have your memory back. It makes everything that much easier."

It's slight, but I feel him still seconds before his mouth is on mine.

His lips are firm and demanding and I have no qualms around reciprocating. Moaning into his mouth, I hold on for dear life as my world tips and shudders being possessed by this man. His tongue plunders and I moan as I hook a leg over his hip and rub. The friction is delicious, the kiss never-ending. Our tongues dance in such a heated way that I'm not sure how I'm still standing. *Oh, wait!* He's holding me up.

My chest rises and falls in time to that of Carter's. His hands are clamped on my bottom as he presses me on his erection. It's the first time I've felt anything like heaven in this way. I grab hold of his head and devour his mouth, our teeth bump together while our hips press and rub.

Breaking away, Carter heavily pants while cursing under his breath. He grips me close so I can no longer move against him, especially the huge rigid penis throbbing into me.

"That wasn't meant to happen," he admits, breathless. "Do you want to come up to my apartment, or should I take you home?" He searches my gaze while he awaits my answer.

I've been ready for him for a while. "Take me to bed, Carter."

His eyes blaze with heat and then we're moving. My feet hardly touch the ground as he rushes us into the building and then the elevator. Inside, he has me pinned to the wall as the elevator moves upward. My legs wrap around his waist.

He hisses into my mouth. "Have you got any idea how much control I'm trying to keep right now?" His eyes darken. "All I want is to tear your panties free and plunge so fucking deep inside of you that I can't feel my fucking toes."

His words melt my insides and send warm arousal directly between my legs. The slow ache that started to build at the beginning of the evening is growing hotter and wetter. I feel swollen down below and need *Carter's* touch.

Panting hard, I throw my head back and moan. "Touch me. Oh God! Carter. Please touch me. I'm burning."

"Fuck!"

We're moving, and after bumps, curses, and hissing, we're inside his dark apartment. The door slams shut, the security lock in place, and then we're off again.

Seconds later, we're falling and bounce slightly as we hit the bed. I kick my shoes off, giggling as Carter struggles to get his shirt off between heated kisses. His arms are stuck in the shirt sleeves as I tug my dress over my shoulders, baring my breasts.

He catches his breath, his mouth capturing a tight nipple. I gasp from the shock and sensation his mouth creates on my flesh as he moves to the other.

His tongue tickles and his mouth sucks, creating pleasure that isn't far off from exploding.

He pops my breast free, growling at how he's restricted by his shirt.

Laughing, he jumps from the bed and ends up ripping the shirt to get it off. I wiggle from my panties and shove them down my legs.

Carter gives a loud rumble from deep in his gut at the sight of me naked and spread out on his bed. "Everything off, Carter. I've waited too long to see every inch of you."

Not needing to be told twice, Carter removes every item of clothing before he crawls between my legs and presses a kiss to my mound. I catch a breath and watch him closely. He gives me a wicked grin before his face disappears. A swipe of his tongue has my hips rising, which he presses back down to the bed with an arm over me. His tongue makes me a quivering wreck with jumbled words tumbling from my mouth.

Reaching for his head, I'm not sure if I want to push him away or hold him to me. It's the latter I end up doing while I thrash and writhe against his face. An explosion starts to roll through me from the tips of my breasts, barreling through my body to where Carter does delicious things with his tongue.

I grip him to me and shout his name, my mind and body taken over with pleasure. Pulsing and shuddering in reaction.

I'm unable to catch a breath as Carter rises above me, the nudge of his penis at my entrance. His eyes are dark and his muscle strain with what I now recognize as need.

My body twitches with little aftershocks as I slide my arms around him and grab his ass. I dig my fingernails into his flesh.

Carter curses and plunges deep.

My eyes widen in shock seconds before pain registers. I concentrate on breathing while Carter breathes heavily in my ear. His body quivers with need, yet he doesn't move, for which I am grateful.

The pain drifts away and I let Carter know this by stroking my fingers over his hips and lightly between our joined bodies. He curses and trembles, his lips brushing mine. "Are you okay?"

"Yes." I smile. "Make love to me."

His forehead drops to mine and he holds my gaze. "Nothing has ever felt as right as it does here with you." With those words spoken, he slowly withdraws his cock and just as slowly plunges deep.

Moaning the faster he moves, pleasure tingles in my blood. Carter dips down and kisses me. Our tongues slide together while our bodies move as one. I wrap my legs around his hips, clinging to him as he adjusts and then thrusts deeper, harder, faster, slamming home so deliciously that my toes curl and another explosion starts to build.

Sweaty and so very sexy, Carter tugs his mouth away just as pure ecstasy barrels through us. He grunts and moans while his cock throbs and jerks, prolonging my own release.

His breathing ragged, Carter momentarily collapses on top of me before he rolls us to our sides. I'm held fast in his arms, neither one of us ready to move away from the other.

23

CARTER

I can't find my voice after such a violent release. Semen poured from me into Addison and there was nothing I could do to stop it. We didn't use protection and I honestly don't care, although I should talk to Addison about it. In all honesty, I had meant to withdraw before coming inside of her, but the feel of her pussy, swollen and wet, clenching as she came with me, blew my mind. Nothing has ever felt as perfect as it has tonight with this woman.

It's on the tip of my tongue to admit that I can't remember the past eight months and that everything I know about her, I got from the girls and my friends. I don't want to fuck up with her, especially after what we've just done. It was her first time too. So, yeah, I'm not fucking this up. I want it perfect for her, not have her running from me because I lied about my memory.

"Are you okay?" I whisper, searching her face.

"I love you, Carter." She nuzzles into my chest. "I wish I'd told you before. I was scared. I'm sorry."

"Hey." I tip her face up to mine. "You have nothing to be sorry about." I smile. "I hope you'll consider moving upstairs now. I'd like you to live here instead of with Bryson."

She grins. "Are you jealous of him?"

"No. I'm way hotter than he is."

"I would have to agree, but don't tell him that. He's been really good to me, Carter." Becoming serious, she adds, "He gave me a home when I had nowhere to go. He's a friend." She grins. "It's been like having a brother. I always wanted one when I was growing up. And now I do."

"I'm glad he helped you when I fucked everything up." I don't say too much in case I give myself away. It's frustrating not being able to remember when I want to remember every moment I've spent with this amazing girl.

One thing I do know is that I love her. Without my recollection of her, something told me that she belonged with me. I'd known something wasn't right.

"I love you too." I kiss the tip of her nose. "I feel as though I've loved you from the moment we met in Duke's." I kiss her cheek before brushing my lips over hers. "Are we okay now?" I ask warily, praying she's forgiven me.

She swallows hard. "Yes. I forgive you." She pauses. "You need to make it clear to *that* girl that she has to stop making shit up regarding you."

"I already did, but I think she needs telling again." I wince. "Forget about her. I'm going to run us a bath."

Moaning, I stretch. "I'm too tired for a bath. The morning."

"You'll be sore."

"I'll be sore either way. Morning." She snuggles deeper while I keep her close.

Overwhelmed with tenderness for this woman, I brush a kiss across her brow and close my eyes.

THE POUNDING ON THE DOOR SURPRISES ME, ALTHOUGH it shouldn't. Bryson will be checking on Addison, no doubt the girls having something to do with that too.

Without looking through the peephole, I yank the door open. "Can you not wait until after break—" The words die in my mouth when I realize Lucy is the early-morning caller.

She bursts into tears and throws herself at me. Startled, I take a step back and curse when she kicks the door closed. "I need you," she wails. "You can't break up with me. You loved me before you got knocked out. We're having a baby." She sniffles. "Do you want me to tell the press you kicked me and your unborn child out?"

I blink a few times, hoping like hell I'm dreaming. Unfortunately, I'm not so lucky because she's still standing before me. She's making the usual crying noises, but no tears are in sight.

I glance at the bedroom door as I put the kitchen counter between us. "Lucy, what the hell is going on?"

"I'm pregnant." She smiles.

"Congratulations," I say. "Do I know the father?"

Her eyes narrow. "It's you!"

I burst out laughing. No way am I letting her put

this on me. I might not have my memory back, but I know I haven't fucked her in the last eight months.

At least you think you haven't.

"I'm not doing this with you," I say, annoyed. "I'm not having you fuck with my life. I told you to stay away from me, and that also goes for Addison. She's the woman I love and the one I want to be with." I stomp to the front door. "Out you go." I wave out into the hallway, which she ignores.

"I'm not going anywhere. We have our baby's arrival to plan."

"And what does that have to do with Carter?" Addison demands, moving closer dressed in my game shirt.

My eyes rove over her, and when I meet her gaze, my world once again rights itself. She's aware Lucy lies.

"You're being unfaithful to me!" Lucy shouts. "How could you when I'm carrying your child?"

"Get over yourself, Lucy. Carter isn't the father. He knows that. I know that. And especially you know that. Also, are you aware there are DNA tests that can be done at an early stage in pregnancy? I'm sure you wouldn't mind undergoing one of those if you're so certain Carter is the father." Addison stares at Lucy, who goes bright red and bursts into tears.

"Carter, are you going to let her talk to me like that? It has nothing to do with her."

Annoyed, I hiss, "It has everything to do with her. Now leave. You're not welcome here."

"Fuck, not again. You're like the plague." Bryson strolls in through the open doorway, takes Lucy's arm, and propels her out into the hallway. "Theo will escort you from the building." The door slams in her face.

I immediately turn to Addison. "I promise it's not me."

She rolls her eyes. "I know. She's a vindictive harlot." She grins. "I bet she isn't even pregnant."

"I wondered that too." Bryson kisses Addison on the cheek before he looks between us.

"You have something else to say?"

Bryson smirks. "Not a thing. However, I did come to see if you both wanted to join us for breakfast." He grins and starts laughing when he sees the annoyance on my face. "I'm joking. Theo spotted Lucy in the elevator across from ours. We figured you might need a bit of help getting rid of her."

"She's a pest," I hiss.

"I'm going to get dressed." Addison saunters off into the bedroom while my eyes follow her. I notice Bryson's do too. The asshole grins.

"I like legs." He shrugs. "She has a nice pair."

"You need to look at someone else's legs." I frown. "I didn't fuck her, did I?"

"Who, Lucy? Hell no!"

"Are you sure? Maybe I didn't tell you."

Bryson frowns and tilts his head. "Carter, you only fucked Lucy once." He pauses. "You're not thinking there is truth in her words, are you?"

"How the fuck do I know when I can't remember," I hiss.

A gasp from the bedroom doorway draws my gaze.

Addison!

Her face looks haunted, and I'm left momentarily speechless. I can't even remember what I was talking to Bryson about.

"You told me you remembered," she says softly, tears in her voice.

Fuck me! Now I remember what Bryson and I were talking about.

"Did you lie to me?"

"I'll be downstairs if you need me." Bryson gets to

the door and says over his shoulder, "Either of you, that is."

I tug at my hair, feeling more stressed than I have in a while. "No, I didn't lie to you. Not about us. Never about us. I love you. I meant every word I said to you." I give her a pleading look. "I don't remember, okay? I just knew when we were in the same room together that there was something there. Something that was unique and special. Camden told me everything he knew. It only made me more desperate to make things right with you. I never lied about only having sex once with Lucy."

"You can't remember though, so how can you say that? You were even questioning yourself with Bryson."

"Because I'm a fucking idiot."

I reach for Addison's hand and feel a sense of relief when she intertwines her fingers with mine. "I remember that I told myself afterward never to be with her again because she was clingy and wanted more. I desperately want to remember everything about my time with you. It kills me that I can't. When I'm with you, I know it's meant to be. I feel that in here." I place her hand over my heart. "Please believe me."

"It ends now, Carter," she says, and my heart plunges to my toes. "I don't mean us," she continues. "I mean the lying. You do not lie to me again, no matter what. Promise me."

"I promise." I kiss her hand and offer her a soft smile. "I was making you breakfast before we were rudely interrupted."

"I don't want breakfast. I just want you."

24

ADDISON

"Come on my cock." Carter pants, pounding into me. "God, Addison. I can't hold off."

"I don't want you to," I hiss as my release thunders through me, my pussy massaging Carter's flesh as he thrusts deep and pours out his pleasure.

Breathing deeply, Carter has his face pressed between my breasts while I feel our joined release soaking us both.

"That was the hottest sex I've ever had."

"I'm not sure I can walk." I giggle, ending with a moan when Carter grabs my hips and slowly slides from me. My pussy clenches hard, trying to keep him inside. Carter curses.

"I could spend all day in this janitor's closest with you, if I didn't have to be on the ice."

He quickly shoves himself away and looks down at me, his eyes momentarily closing. Grabbing some paper towels, he dries between my legs and helps me dress. By the time he's done, my body tingles for more.

After two weeks of lots and lots of sex, our bodies are well tuned to each other's pleasure. We can't keep our hands off the other, which is how we ended up in the janitor's closet.

"You can have as much of me as you can take later." Carter grins, giving me a wink.

I raise a brow. "I look forward to it.

He laughs and kisses me on the cheek, then he takes my hand. "We better go."

"Hmm," I mutter, trying to stop my cheeks from flaming at what we've been up to.

Carter opens the door and stumbles. "What the fuck are you doing standing there?" he snarls.

I shove him out of the doorway and feel my cheeks flame hotter.

"Hello, Addison."

Inwardly groaning, I plaster a smile on my face. "Hi, Ethan."

"Stop embarrassing her," Riley says, moving toward me. "Tell the big man you'll see him after practice," she says and wraps an arm around mine.

"How do you know how big he is?" Ethan frowns at his wife.

She snickers. "I was referring to his height. What did you think I meant, husband?"

Ethan narrows his eyes before he laughs. "Go and gossip. I need a word with Carter."

Riley pulls me away, tittering. "That was funny. I bet he's big," she says. "Is he?"

I open my mouth, but nothing comes out. I clear my throat, and say, "That's none of your business."

"Spoilsport. I'll admit that Ethan is hung rather nicely."

"Oh God, you're going to make me say it, huh? Okay, Carter is huge. Happy now?"

She laughs. "You are so funny."

"Never mind me being funny. Did I notice Ethan's boot was off?"

"You did! He has a brace on now and must do physio, but otherwise he's on the mend. He'll be back on the ice soon."

"That's good." I frown. "Where are we going?"

"To meet the girls." She pauses. "Well, not Molly. She's busy."

We're exiting the arena at this point, and I freeze in shock. My father is walking toward us, pushing Maureen in the wheelchair, and my stomach turns. He scared me to death last time I saw him.

"Who is that with Maureen?" Riley asks quietly.

"My dad."

"Do you want me to wait in the car?" Riley offers, concern for me written all over her face.

I shake my head. "Stay with me, please."

"You got it."

"Addison," my father says in an apologetic voice. I must remind myself that we've been here before.

"Why are you both here?"

Maureen twitches, but my father is the one to reply. "We are leaving the city. Going to Pennsylvania. It will be quieter there. Maureen and her parents are coming too. It's a new start and we thought we'd give you one last chance to come with us." His eyes search mine and I offer him a smile, feeling an overwhelming relief.

"Thank you, but I have to decline. My life is here in Boston with my friends and the man I love." I hold my father's furious gaze. "I love him, Father. He loves me. I'm not leaving, but I wish you, Mother, and Maureen's family all the best in your new home."

"That's it?" Maureen snarls. "You put me in this chair and walked away."

"We both know the first part of that is not true. Even my father knows that." I stare at my father until he looks away.

I grip Riley's arm and whisper, "Get me out of here."

"Gladly." To my father, she says, "We have to go." Ushering me to her truck, I don't take a steady breath until she's driving us away.

"He's intense."

"You have no idea," I mutter, and glance out the back window. "We're out of view." My heart pounds and blood thunders through my ears. "I'm relieved they're moving. Very much so."

"Relax. It's over with."

I nod and close my eyes, letting the soft hum of the engine settle me while my mind wanders toward the surprise Carter has for me.

25

CARTER

FEELING SATED, I JOIN THE TEAM ON THE ICE AND GET a dark glare from Coach. I make quick work of my skates and jump on the ice before Coach can reach me. His sharp Russian cursing reaches me though.

I skate past him and shout, "Sorry I'm late. Had something to take care of."

Van continues to scowl while Bennett nudges me with his stick. "I'm sure you meant someone." He wiggles his brows.

I smirk. "As though you've never taken Scarlett in this building."

"I'm the captain." He laughs. "I'm allowed."

He gets the finger.

I give my all to training this afternoon. Speed and

agility are two things a player needs to do what we do. Not as a one-off, but daily. The Vikings are a good team on and off the ice. It can feel like having a huge family with how some of the players butt into each other's lives. But I wouldn't wish for it to be any different.

Talk about butting in, Ivan has kept to himself, which isn't like him. Sure, he can be a loner, but he usually practices his defense tactics on us poor suckers. Today he's hardly looked at anyone.

Catching Bryson's eye, I nod toward the big Russian. Bry shakes his head, which of course I ignore.

Ivan eyes me warily as I approach. "I do not want to talk like a woman."

I roll my eyes. "We're family. We talk. Spit it out."

"Spit what out?" He frowns.

"Cut that shit out and tell me what is going on with you. Is it the visa?" Camden had also filled me in on Ivan's current situation.

"*Da!*"

Okay, we're getting somewhere. "What about the visa?"

"A friend of Boss, he gets permission for my mother and sister to visit America."

My eyes widen. "That's great news!"

"Nyet."

"Why not?" I sigh. "Ivan, it's like trying to get blood from a stone talking to you."

"I do not want Anya marrying a player."

What the hell is he talking about?

Then it clicks. I burst out laughing. Ivan gives me a dark look. "Anya and your mother are safe from the Vikings, Ivan. I can't imagine anyone being into an arranged marriage. Besides, none of us want to be married to you."

"*Blyad!*" Ivan hisses under his breath.

"I know you said fuck."

Ivan glares. "My sister is nothing like me. She is a good girl."

"Your apartment isn't big enough, so where are they staying?"

He sighs and finally gives me a look for help.

Becoming serious, I say, "Look, none of us want you taken from us. Believe it or not, we consider you family."

Ivan nods.

I swallow. "We need a team meeting to discuss how we can help you."

"It is not good. Payton said she will miss me."

"Wait, what? Who's Payton? What'd I miss?"

"Payton work at the diner. She talks to me." He frowns. "She's a nice girl."

I grin. "Do you have a crush on her, Ivan?" I tease, and he narrows his eyes.

Backing away, I hold up my hands...then it happens, memory overload. I rapidly blink and feel Ivan take a strong hold of my arm.

"Carter?"

I reach out and grip the rink side, sliding down until I'm sitting on the ice. My head pounds, but I remember. Everything. My fuckup with Addison and how I was feeling let down that night. I remember that I did, in fact, only ever sleep with Lucy the one time. I also remember the heartbroken look on Addison's face when she caught me with Lucy, and the indecision running through me at the time.

The face of Doc Clive wavers in my vision before I get a clearer view. "What happened?"

"I'm fine. I got my memory back."

Doc pauses. "You got your memory back while riling Ivan up?" He laughs. "Okay, then," he drawls. "I do want to check you out fully though."

"Yeah," I agree. "Can someone haul my ass from the ice?"

Ivan grabs me up and holds me steady while I find my feet.

"Thanks," I mutter. I meet Ivan's gaze and add, "We're going to fight for you, Ivan."

Theo and Bryson cover me as I leave the ice, probably making sure I don't drop like a sack of bricks.

After sitting for a few and shoving my sneakers back on my feet, I feel fine. I guzzle the bottle of water Camden passes over.

"Fuck," I mutter, noticing Lucy on her way over.

Theo says, "When will you give up?"

"He's the father of my baby, so I won't be giving up anytime soon."

"Court," I blurt, exasperated with the woman. "We'll go to court and let the judge order a paternity test and choose the clinic. When the result comes back that I'm not the father, you can cover the cost of court. I'll make sure my attorney requests that." I smirk at the surprise on Lucy's face. "I know I'm not the father because I remember every damn thing." I lean closer. "Everything, Lucy. So if you have thousands of dollars to waste, then let me know and I'll see you in court. Otherwise, leave me the hell alone."

"You're an asshole." She turns and stomps away.

"Do you really remember everything about her?" Bryson asks.

"I do. I have a lot to make up for with Addison." I sigh and slouch down in the seat so I can rest my head. I gaze up at the ceiling. "I love her. Addison. She's a breath of fresh air, and I fucking love her. I need to make a grand gesture so she knows how special she is."

Her pretty face comes into view, and I blink a few times, but no, she's still there. She grins. "I think I know how special I am."

Jumping to my feet, I end up tossing water in Theo's crotch, and only stay on my feet because of Bryson's strong hold on my shirt.

Laughing, Addison slips past Bryson once I'm steady on my feet and cups my face. "Are you being truthful this time? You remember everything?"

"Yes. I remember the diner, walking you to work. I remember the fuckup I made of everything. I remember how much my heart hurt because of what I did to you." I lift her up into my arms. "I love you."

"Good." She smacks a kiss on me in front of my teammates that makes my fucking toes curl.

EPILOGUE – CARTER

This afternoon is a fun skate with a group of school kids. These tend to be light entertainment for the kids, and they watch us goofing around on the ice. They watch us play and then it's their turn on the ice with us shadowing them. They're always eager with excitement at getting to skate with us, even the kids who support different teams. It's a sport and we'll assist and encourage anyone interested in furthering their skills.

Dallas, Wyatt's live-in partner, coaches kids' hockey and is good at spotting who to push upward.

Molly is down here, helping herd the kids toward the skates that she prearranged to be at the rink. Riley is booted up to help on the ice with Ethan keeping watch. I don't know why he hovers when she's on the ice because Riley can skate better than him. Not that I'll ever admit that. Scarlett, Hailee, and Addison help fasten the boots on along with the kids' teacher, Emery.

"What's up with Bry?" Theo nudges my shoulder.

"The girl is his niece, Anna."

"That isn't what I meant."

I face Theo and frown. "What did you mean?"

"Haven't you seen him gawking at the teacher, who is doing her best to ignore him?"

"Ah!" I chuckle. "That must be the teacher who Bryson's niece overheard telling another teacher he was a player."

Theo snorts with amusement. "He's a fucking nun." Skating away, he continues to watch, saying something to Noah, who glances their way.

Ignoring the antics and gossip of my teammates, I skate toward the kids, making sure I stop close to where Addison is.

Her cheeks and the tip of her nose are rosy from the cold coming from the ice, but she doesn't care. She's happy. Her face lights up as she turns and finds me ogling her butt in her tight jeans.

"What are you looking at?"

I grin. "My girl." I reach out and catch the ends of her scarf, gently pulling her closer. "My everything girl."

"I like that." Going up on tiptoes, she wraps her arms around my neck and presses her lips to mine.

Growling, I quickly hold her to me and deepen the kiss. At least, I try to deepen the kiss.

Addison pulls away and gives me a teasing smile. "I love you," she says before blowing me a kiss.

My heart races.

I'm going to marry that woman.

THE END

Thank you for reading *Carter: on the ice,* and thank you for your reviews! It's really appreciated.

Subscribe with your email to be alerted about new releases, sales, and events.

http://ronajameson.com

STRYKER SUMMARY
WRITTEN AS LEXI BUCHANAN

When my childhood friend, Cora, dared me to write a sexy novel about a martial arts fighter, I agreed, albeit under the influence of alcohol. It was something for me—something different and exciting.

It was supposed to be research, pure and simple. But then I met him—a six-foot-six mountain of a man with no name. The way his muscles flexed and rippled when he trained made my belly quiver. The way his dark hair flopped over his forehead made me want to brush it back from his strong face. His nose had been broken, but it made no difference, he was still a handsome man. He had eyes dark as the night that would land on me the minute I entered his gym…Every…Time.

He was their star fighter, the one that brought in the big money. At first I feared him because of his size and the way he would look at me. But then I discovered that I was his biggest distraction, and no matter what my head told me, my heart told me to fight for the man who didn't know how to live outside of the cage.

NYT & USA Today bestselling author Lexi Buchanan brings you her new sexy standalone novel about fighting for freedom when the odds are against you.

Stryker (10 years ago)

"Dad, I'm not sure this is such a good idea." My heart raced in my chest as though it would explode. My palms went slick as fear coursed through my veins.

I'd already thought Dad's late night plans were a bad idea…and they seemed worse the minute I saw the dark, deserted alley. It gave me the chills.

Nothing good was up that alley.

Even at fourteen I knew it, but my dad was determined so I followed him across the street. Something shouted for me to run, which gave me pause, but my legs had a mind of their own and followed him.

My dad turned, and then frowned when he

noticed the slight hesitation in my usual eagerness to follow him anywhere. The nervous twitch in his right eye went crazy. "It isn't, but it's the only thing I can do."

Before I could work out what he meant, my dad grabbed my arm as though he was afraid I'd run. He dragged me to the mouth of what I considered a nightmare.

The stench of rotten food made me want to hurl. Every creak, even the wind howling around us, had my eyes constantly straining to see through the pitch black. I half expected someone to jump out brandishing a gun, or knife, or some other weapon.

Head down, my eyes landed on the hold my dad had on my arm. Something wasn't right. In fact, nothing about the evening felt right.

I knew my dad constantly bet on the fighters in the cage, winning and losing on a regular basis, but what that had to do with tonight, if anything, I didn't know. My dad never took me to the fights no matter how much I begged. I wanted to hang out with dad... wanted to be like the fighters—tough, strong, fearless. One day, that would be me standing in the cage with the crowds shouting my name. Then my dad wouldn't have any choice about keeping me away from that life.

I'd never understood the obsession my dad had for the fights, but they'd put him on a high for days afterwards…unless he lost.

Pulled to a stop, I felt the shake of my dad's hand as his grip tightened. He turned to look at me and the fear I saw in his eyes was something I'd never expected to see. My blood turned to ice and the wrongfulness of the night felt all too real as a large vehicle headed down the alley from the opposite entrance.

Caught in the headlights, my first reaction was to run and hide. The tension jumping off my dad was high. His breathing was frantic and sweat beaded on his forehead.

With my free hand, I shoved the black hood of my sweatshirt from my head so I didn't miss anything.

My pulse hammered in my neck and all I could hear was my heartbeat thrashing in my ears.

When my dad's only reaction was to stand and stare at the approaching vehicle, I knew then, that they where here because of him.

What had he done?

"Dad?" I turned and hoped he'd offer me an explanation as fear and anger knotted in my gut.

He didn't and wouldn't meet my gaze until the purr of the SUV's engine cut off. "Son, I'm sorry. If there was any other way I'd have taken it, but there isn't...I love you. You won't believe those words soon, but I mean them with every breath I take."

"What?"

Before he could say more, the doors of the SUV opened and a large man climbed out, moving behind us. Three other men emerged and stood in front.

The one in a dark suit stepped forward, his steely eyes on my dad. "Peter."

"Mr—"

"No names tonight...*Peter*." His gaze slid to me and my breath caught at the back of my throat. He looked me over—assessing. "He'll do."

What did he mean?

"Dad?"

My dad didn't explain and, seconds later, I felt his grip on my arm loosen as the large guy stepped closer.

None of this made any sense, but I'd known something was wrong the minute I'd stepped out of our apartment.

It was obvious that my dad had done, said, or agreed to something, but my brain worked overtime trying to work out just what.

Then I felt my wrists clasped tightly before they were pulled behind my back in a grip so strong that I knew even as I struggled that I wouldn't get free.

"Dad," I shouted, my eyes begged him to help me, but he just watched while they dragged me away.

The suit held his hand out and halted the guy who had me. He spoke with a threat inflected into his voice to my dad, "With this exchange, you can consider your debt paid in full. You stay away from him and me, and, you never step foot near the cage again…in any city. You won't like the consequences if you do." The man in the dark suit stepped in close to my dad, and threatened, "Am I clear?"

My dad's body quivered in fear and his eyes nearly bugged out of his head while the man threatened him.

Fear trickled from my belly and gradually spread throughout the more I listened to the conversation around me.

Until now, I had no idea just how serious my dad's gambling habit had become. I should have though. But surely he wasn't giving me over to the men to settle his debt. Was he? What did they want with me?

What... No!

The hold on me tightened as I started to struggle. The man behind me wasn't like the others. He was big and strong, and wore jeans and shirt as opposed to the others in suits. His scent was trouble, and even though I continued to struggle, I knew that he wouldn't release me.

My heart pounded as sweat ran down my face, mingling with the tears I couldn't control as my situation sank into my brain.

My dad, who I loved, who I thought loved me, had sold me in exchange for his gambling debt to be wiped clean. How could he do that?

My dad glanced at me one last time, pain in his eyes, before he turned and ran down the alley.

The man behind, tugged me toward a black SUV, but I struggled and tried to dig in my heels, my eyes still on my dad as he ran and left me with these assholes.

At the SUV, another man tried to grab my legs, but I kicked out and heard him curse as my booted foot slammed into the man's jaw.

"Hold that fucker," the man growled, grabbing me around the neck while more hands held me down.

My vision started to dim but then the man in

charge forcibly removed the hands. "I don't want the fucker dead." He stepped back straightening his jacket. "Get him in the truck. *Now.*"

No way!

In a last ditched effort to get away, I yelled, *"Dad! Help me!"*

My dad paused.

They all did.

Then my dad took one step toward me…hesitated. A bullet hissed from beside me—a silencer muffled the sound—and I watched as my dad disappeared around the corner seconds before I saw brick from the building fly off.

He did it!

He left me!

"I'm not going with you," I raged against everything. The fact of what my dad had done, the restraints holding my wrists, the hands gripping me. I struck out, blindly, as I struggled and kicked. My teeth sank into the soft flesh of the hand covering my mouth and I felt a moment of triumph as the man cursed in pain. Seconds later, the triumph was gone as the man's fist flew into my face. I felt the pain blossom, starting on my nose as my mouth filled with the metallic taste of blood. The pain ricocheted through me as I turned my head to the side and spat out blood. It felt like my jaw was on fire while I breathed through the pain.

I sucked in a breath to fight harder but my body tensed as fingers dug into my cheeks as a hand clamped around my face. The man in charge leaned forward, his eyes burning with anger as he loomed over me. "You're mine now lad. You're going to become my fighting machine. No more fucking nursemaids. I'm going to make you a man, and you're going to make me money to pay off your father's debt."

I couldn't talk with the hand clamped around me, but I memorized the man's face, and made sure that I would never forget it.

That close to me I noticed the scar to the right side of his face that ran a good few inches. I thought that he was an American at first, but now I wasn't sure. Something else was in him, and his accent, one I couldn't place, slipped with his anger.

I hoped that when I woke up in the morning the memory of tonight would still be there. Because one day, when I was a man—stronger—I was going to get even with everyone involved...including my dad, the one person I always thought would be there to love and support me—the one person who was supposed to protect me from evil.

How wrong was I?

Evie (10 years ago)

While my mom and dad were partying with friends, and supporters of my father, I was on the sidelines trying to pretend my life didn't suck. I'd tried to fake a headache so I'd be allowed to stay home but it hadn't worked. I'd been told to sit and sip water regardless as to how late it had gotten.

I was twelve years old and hated that my father had just been elected as a state senator. My mother told me that I was selfish for thinking about myself all the time; that I should be more supportive.

How could I be more supportive when the new job meant my father would be away from home even more than he already had been? I really didn't see me wanting my dad at home as being selfish. I loved him, and missed him when he wasn't home.

But now, he would be gone more and school would be even harder to deal with. The other kids loved to make fun of me because of my family and my father's ambition.

I wanted to be part of a normal family. I couldn't even remember the last time we all ate around the table at the same time. I would only have my dad for family vacations now. He'd promised more but I knew that wouldn't happen. He loved his work, and really I should stop being ungrateful because I had everything I would ever want...apart from the one thing I *really* wanted...my father home.

My one best friend, Millie, was the only one who truly knew my fears, and she was the only person to know how much I hated my life.

Over the past few months I'd spent so much time at Millie's house that it felt like my second home. I loved being there. Her father was larger than life and, although he'd scared me at first, I'd finally gotten used to him.

My mother still tried to keep me apart from Millie when she wasn't lost in a world of her own making, and actually paid more attention as to what I was up to.

Like now.

I sighed as I spotted her walking toward me with a sour expression on her face, as though she'd eaten a lemon. It soon changed to a smile when Mrs. Grant appeared to her right.

Mom certainly had something on her mind though because her path continued toward me. I hated being center of attention, which she knew so I hoped that I wasn't expected on stage or anything while my father made his speech, even though I knew I wouldn't get away without.

"Evie dear." Mom took the cup of water from my hand and tugged me up. "Straighten your dress. Your father is about to make his speech and we both need to be at his side to show our support." And then she had to go and ruin it all. "We'll be on the front page of the newspaper tomorrow."

My heart sank and I wanted to run. I would have except her grip around my wrist tightened…almost to the point of being painful.

"Just be pleasant for the rest of the night, and," her lips twisted with annoyance, "I'll let you go on the trip with Millie and her family."

While her words sunk into my shocked brain, I let her lead me across the room to where my father stood with his team.

Mom knew how to get her way but I didn't for one minute believe she'd just thought about that to get me to do their bidding. She'd have something else up her sleeve and need me out of the way so that she didn't have a child to supervise. I wasn't about to complain because I wanted to go to Chicago with Millie more than anything. When I'd brought it up to Mom, she'd scoffed at the idea because she considered Millie's family beneath her. I couldn't see why she couldn't treat everyone the same.

"Smile," she hissed between her teeth.

And like the world's most lifelike puppet, I did exactly what she wanted. My smile was full of love and support as we greeted Father.

"There she is." His smile was real as he enclosed me in his warm embrace and I felt a pang of guilt that mine wasn't. "My princess," he whispered against my ear before he kissed the top of my head.

Available at ALL online retailers.

TEARS IN THE RAIN SUMMARY
WRITTEN AS RONA JAMESON

Tears.

That's all I had now, tears in the rain, all because I fell in love with a boy.

Growing up, he was always by my side—unmovable—even when his friends teased him. He always knew when I needed him closer. I'd wake from nightmares to find myself wrapped safely in his strong arms. I even asked him to teach me how to kiss a boy, and our love grew into something it never should have—*something forbidden*.

My name is Fallon Scott and this is my story.

Available at ALL online retailers.

SUMMER AT ROSE COTTAGE SUMMARY
WRITTEN AS RONA JAMESON

Love and family transcend time.

Set in the beautiful coastal town of Cape Elizabeth, Maine, 'Summer at Rose Cottage' explores two love stories—one lost in time and the other flourishing in the present. McKenzie (Mack) Harper needs to get away and the small cottage just outside of Cape Elizabeth is the perfect location to unwind and bond with her six-year-old nephew, Lucas. It's here at this quaint summer rental that Mack discovers a diary dated March 4th, 1947, which pulls her into a world of love and heartache.

Each entry into the diary is brought to life through the words written by nineteen-year-old, Rose Degan, who falls in love with a man her parents disapprove of. Her heart knows what and whom it wants, Jacob Evans, a fire fighter in Cape Elizabeth. He hasn't been in town long when they meet on the cliffs while she watches the rescue of a crew from a collier ship that went aground during a fierce storm.

Back in the present, Mack discovers that Jacob is still alive and tries to find him. She leaves a message that falls into the hands of Jacob's grandson, Dean Evans. With his curiosity piqued, Dean decides that the mystery woman, along with her diary, is an excellent excuse to slip away from home, earning a break from his mother's matchmaking shenanigans—a grandchild being her sole focus.

All these characters come together in a story of love and friendship. It shows that love and family can transcend time.

Available at ALL online retailers.

OTHER BOOKS BY AUTHOR

SUMMER 2022

Stohrm Vellis, a fifth realm novel - Lexi writing as Rona Jameson

NEW SERIES - Boston Bay Vikings

Book 1: Camden: on the ice

Book 2: Bennett: on the ice

Book 3: Ethan: on the ice

Book 4: Sutton: on the ice

Book 5: Carter: on the ice

Book 6: Bryson: on the ice

Book 7: Ivan: on the ice

Book 8: Theo: on the ice

Book 9: Noah: on the ice

NEW SERIES - Blossom Creek

Book 1: Christmas at Emelia's

Book 2: A Rake in Blossom Creek

Book 3: Heatwave in Blossom Creek

Book 4: Secret Love in Blossom Creek

De La Fuente Family (McKenzie Spinoff)

Book 1: Love in Montana (Sylvia & Eric)

Book 2: Love in Purgatory (Dante & Emelia)

Book 3: Love in Bloom (Mateo & Erin)

Book 4: Love in Country (Aiden & Sarah)

Book 5: Love in Flame (Diego & Rae)

Book 6: Love in Game (Kasey & Felicity)

Book 7: Love in Education (Andie & Seth)

McKenzie Cousins

(McKenzie Spinoff)

Book 1: Baby Makes Three (Sirena & Garrett)

Book 2: A Business Decision (Michael & Brooke)

Book 3: Secret Kisses (Charlotte & Tanner)

Book 4: Kissing Cousins (Rachel & Alexander)

Book 5: If Only (Madison & Derek)

Book 6: Princess & the Puck (Paige & Seth)

Book 7: A Bakers Delight (Sofia & Shane)

Book 8: A Cowboy for Christmas (Olivia & Geary)

Book 9: A Secret Affair (Joshua & Mallory)

Book 10: One Christmas (Dylan & Jenna)

Book 11: The Pregnant Professor (Jaxon & Poppy)

Book 12: It Started with a Kiss (Ryan & Gretchen)

Jackson Hole

Book 1: From This Moment

Book 1.5: When we Meet (Novella, in the back of From This Moment)

Book 2: New Beginning (coming soon)

Romantic Suspense

Lawful

Stryker

Standalone Novella's

One Dance

Educate Me

Pure

Holiday Season

Kissing Under the Mistletoe

A Soldier's Christmas

Jingle Bells

Written as Rona Jameson

Butterfly Girl

Come Back to Me

Summer at Rose Cottage

Tears in the Rain

Twenty Eight Days

ACKNOWLEDGEMENTS

Editors: Nadine Winningham

Proofreaders: Nadine Winningham and Lynne Garlick

ABOUT THE AUTHOR

English born Rona Jameson is an author of romance who currently resides in Ireland with her husband, four children, one dog and one cat. She's been writing since 2013 as Lexi Buchanan, which is where you can find her more explicit writing.

Follow on social media:

Website: http://ronajameson.com
Email: authorlexibuchanan@gmail.com

- facebook.com/lexibuchananauthor
- twitter.com/AuthorLexi
- instagram.com/authorlexib
- bookbub.com/author/lexi-buchanan
- amazon.com/Lexi-Buchanan/e/B009SPA94U

Made in the USA
Middletown, DE
16 March 2023

26867636R00116